ASSIGNMENT GAOLBREAK

The body of a man, recently sprung from Wormwood Scrubs, is found in a burst-open crate being loaded aboard a ship in Shoreham Docks.

James Packard, London operator for Criminal Warfare Agencies of New York, is assigned to find out the background and to prevent the murder of another convict who is on the run, both from the police, and from his own mob. Packard's enquiries take him from Scotland to Naples, where he eventually catches up with his man!

ASSIGNMENT GAOLBREAK

ASSIGNMENT GAOLBREAK

by

Philip McCutchan

Dales Large Print Books
Long Preston, North Yorkshire, England.

British Library Cataloguing in Publication Data.

McCutchan, Philip
    Assignment gaolbreak.

    A catalogue record for this book is
    available from the British Library

    ISBN 1-85389-474-5 pbk

First published in Great Britain by Robert Hale Ltd., 1968

Copyright © 1968 by Philip McCutchan

The right of Philip McCutchan to be identified as the author
of this work has been asserted by him in accordance with
the Copyrights, Designs and Patents Act, 1988

Published in Large Print 1994 by arrangement with the
copyright holder.

Dales Large Print is an imprint of
Library Magna Books Ltd.
Printed and bound in Great Britain by
T.J. Press (Padstow) Ltd., Cornwall, PL28 8RW.

ONE

It was a threatening day, with much heavy black cloud lying along the line of the Downs from Worthing to Brighton, and gulls wheeling inland over the docks at Shoreham. There was more than a hint of heavy rain to come and the air was close and sultry, the sea outside the breakwater as smooth as glass and with a curious green light on it. Coal dust lay thick and dirty along the dockside, spreading from where a collier from the North of England was discharging to the South-Eastern Electricity Board's Brighton power station. A gang of dockers was working a Norwegian dry-cargo vessel some way along to the west of the collier and they, too, were suffering from the flying coal dust that found its way into throats and eyes, ears and noses. They kept looking up at that lowering, ugly sky, as if wishing for the rain to come and damp down the dust—and give them the excuse to pack up work so they could play cards in one of the big cargo sheds at full Union rates of pay.

The rain came soon enough.

Big heavy drops, just a few to begin with, splashed onto the dockside, onto the decks of the Norwegian. The air was very still and sounds carried a long way until the roll of thunder came close behind a vivid crackle of lightning that seemed to hang right above the tall chimneys of the power station. One of the dockers, a big man with a wide-brimmed hat and an Australian accent, called out, 'Smoke-oh,' and stuck his cargo hook into a handy crate. He and the rest of the gang were beating it for the nearest shed when the next jag of lightning crackled overhead and struck the crane, which happened to have lifted a sling containing four heavy crates all ready to go down into the Norwegian's fore hold. That lightning bent the jib of the crane and fried the driver and broke the cable where it ran over the pulley on the end of the jib.

As the man with the Australian accent yelled an unnecessary warning to his mates and ran like a hare, the sling swooped downwards and crashed its load onto the ship's bulwarks. Two of the crates fell on deck, the other two on the dockside. All of them had split open by the time the

8

dockers emerged from the shed for a look-see. Because of the longer drop, the two that had hit the jetty had split the worse. They had discharged their contents under the cloudburst and among the dancing, bouncing slashes of rain that almost formed a carpet, lay shattered electronic equipment and transistor radios. But there was something else there as well and the Australian was the first to spot it.

'It's a bloke,' he said. He sounded puzzled. 'No one standing out where that lot fell, was there, eh?'

He ran forward, looking up at the tottering jib of the crane as he did so. 'Could be Ted, poor bastard,' he said. Ted had been the crane driver. But what the Australian found when he reached the spot wasn't Ted. It had been a bloke once, right enough, but now it was a very dead corpse, stare-eyed and waxen and naked, grotesque and obscene beneath that pelting downpour and the vivid streaks of lightning that still played around the power station's chimneys.

James Packard put his hands flat on Felicity Teal's desk and bent down to kiss the top of her honey-coloured hair.

He knew she liked that, though she always pretended she didn't in working hours. It was just that she was scared Forbes might come in and catch her, and she had a naïve idea, and Packard found this quite appealing, that Forbes didn't know the set-up between his secretary and Criminal Warfare Agencies' Number One London operator. Packard saw the blush on her face when he stepped back. He grinned and said, 'All right, Felicity, I'll behave for now. What is it this time?'

The girl patted at her hair, looked coy, and straightened her shoulders and the neckline of her dress when she saw the angle of Packard's gaze. Really, she thought, there was no need for him to look at her like that in the office...she had been warned by her predecessor, a girl named Suzy, about James Packard, and for a while she had heeded the warning, which had included the information that James Packard, though a nice enough man, and generous, wasn't the sort to look to for marriage since he had too much of the wandering streak in him; but she hadn't been able to keep her distance because she had found that James Packard switched her on more than any man she had ever met...

'Come back from your dream world,' Packard said now, 'and tell me what it's all about?'

'Oh, sorry,' she said. 'It's the body in Shoreham docks. Down in Sussex. Haven't you read about it?'

Packard nodded and yawned. 'Yes, but I haven't been paying much attention. Has something blown up?'

She said, 'You might say that. Veldcamp, Beerman and MacLaren have been on to Colonel Forbes.'

'About the body?'

'Yes.'

'Who are they, anyway?'

'Veldcamp, Beerman and MacLaren? They're diamond merchants. Don't you remember—the Hatton Garden robbery?'

'Oh, yes,' Packard said. 'Yes, I do. They asked us to find the loot, didn't they? And so far we haven't. Around a million quid's worth. Well, well! So what's the link, Felicity darling?'

She was just about to say she didn't know when the intercom buzzed at her and she pressed a switch and said, 'Yes, Colonel Forbes,' and Forbes's harsh voice barked at her to send Packard in.

'I'm on my way,' he said. 'See you.' He

11

moved across to the door and knew the girl was watching him as he did so. She'd told him once she liked his walk; there was something elemental in it, she'd said, but hadn't been able to explain further than that, which left him to guess. In Forbes's room he nodded at the spare, neatly-moustached ex-soldier behind the desk and dropped into a chair facing him.

Filling his pipe Forbes asked, 'What has Miss Teal told you?'

'Only that it concerns the Shoreham docks body...and Veldcamp, Beerman and—'

'Right. Now, you'll have gathered from the papers that the body had been packed into a crate that burst open. I don't suppose you know yet whose body that was.'

Packard said, 'I haven't a clue. Have you?'

'Yes. I know exactly who it was, and so do the police, but nothing's being allowed to leak yet. That corpse was Robert Morrissey, alias Gerald Copeman, alias The Big Peter. Got it?'

'Got it,' Packard said, stretching out his long legs across the deep pile of the carpet. 'And I think I've got the link with the firm with the funny name, too. Wasn't it Morrissey who was the peterman in the Hatton Garden robbery?'

Forbes nodded. 'Correct, James. You'll also know, I imagine, that he was sprung from the Scrubs last year?'

'I did read about it, yes. So?'

'So he's dead! Now, if you'll cast your mind back, James, you'll remember the police suspected that job was organised, or anyway carried out, by around a dozen men—but they only ever got a smell of six. Those six would never talk, so no more arrests were made. Somewhere, someone is sitting pretty. Sitting nice and safe, too. And that someone is now organising the springing of the birds inside. Something else you may remember is that another of the six, Brett Burgoyne, was sprung a couple of months ago from Wandsworth. Now, why do men on the safe side of the prison bars stick their necks out to help their colleagues escape, James? Can you tell me that?'

Packard said, 'Well, there can be several reasons. The Old Pal's Act, for one. Oh, I know that's doubtful—'

'In the case of this particular mob, it's right out of the reckoning. They're

13

vicious—*really* vicious. I'd also reject any idea that they may be honouring some kind of pact, a deal made before the robbery that they'd all look after one another if anybody got the chop. They may well have made such a deal, but I'm damned sure the Sibley Boys, which is what they call themselves, would never honour it. Not with a million pounds sterling involved. No, James, we need to look elsewhere for the answer this time.'

Packard nodded thoughtfully. 'Think they're trying to stop any talking that might come, now half the mob's had a longish spell inside?'

'Somehow I doubt that,' Forbes said. He blew smoke across the room; it trailed into expensive curtains. 'Neither Morrissey nor Burgoyne was the sort to grass. There's another angle that comes to my mind, and it's this: none of that loot was ever found, not even in Holland, where at least some of it was believed to have gone via the fences. And enquiries have revealed that both Morrissey and Burgoyne's families have been living pretty well since the robbery. Not too flashy—they wouldn't be taking too obvious a risk—but well enough and certainly much better than the breadwinners' station in life could ever hope to have provided for legitimately. Now, I'm aware that *could* mean that the Sibley Boys do look after their own to that extent. But—it could also mean, James, that both Morrissey and Burgoyne hid their share away where no one else can get at it.'

'And now the Sibley Boys are in need of more cash...what with devaluation and credit squeezes and all?' Packard grinned.

Forbes said, 'Yes. That's what it could be. And now Morrissey's dead.'

'Quite. But what puzzles me is...why get rid of the body—or rather as it turned out *not* get rid of the body—that way? I'd have thought they could have found better ways—acid baths, heavy weights in the Channel, dismembering and scattering—that sort of thing?'

Forbes pointed out, 'All those methods have their practical drawbacks, as you well know. Haigh tried the acid bath and got caught, heavy weights can come adrift, tides throw up bodies, inquisitive children find thigh bones. The method they used would have worked if it hadn't been for sheer bad luck. That crate had passed customs and it would never have been queried again. And they may have wanted the body kept intact—to impress somebody else who wouldn't talk, but who would open up like an oyster if faced with a fellow double-crosser's corpse.'

'Burgoyne?'

'Exactly—Brett Burgoyne! So what I want you to do is prevent another murder. Find Burgoyne before he joins Morrissey! Even if Burgoyne decides to talk about where he stashed his share of the loot, he's still going to be too dangerous to leave in this world, James.'

'But do we, let's face it, really want to keep him in it?'

Forbes shrugged. 'I know what you mean. A night-watchman died in that Hatton Garden job—'

'Yes. After a very nasty beating up.'

Forbes sighed and said, 'It might be all Burgoyne deserves, but we still can't permit another preventable murder. Anyway, it's not up to us to query the Home Office, and it's the Home Secretary himself who's asked us to take this on—independently of the police.'

Packard raised an eyebrow. 'How do the police feel about that one?' he asked.

Forbes grinned. 'The same as they

always feel, I expect.' He reached into a drawer. 'You'd better take a look at some rather good photographs of Burgoyne,' he said, and passed them across. Burgoyne, Packard noted, had a dark, Mediterranean look—handsome, in a somewhat Italian or Spanish fashion. Not that it helped much...

As he was leaving the office suite to pick up the Ferrari, Felicity Teal called after him, 'Earlier on, James, you said "see you." Did that mean anything, or not?'

'It meant exactly what it said, darling. No time limit specified.' He saw the sudden disappointment in her eyes so he added, 'No promises, but if I'm free I'll call for you around eight and we'll go somewhere for a meal. How's that?'

'Lovely,' she said.

TWO

Like all things the execution of which was clearly going to be extremely difficult, this job *sounded* straightforward enough. Find Brett Burgoyne. Just like that. At first

17

sight the imprisoned elements of the Sibley outfit seemed the most suitable persons for a softening-up process that might yield a few general leads, but it was pretty doubtful, on deeper thought, that they would really come across with anything worth while. If they'd been inclined to talk, something would have emerged by now, something that would have reached the governors of the prison where they were being held. As for the rest of the Sibley mob, those outside—they would hardly be susceptible to any frontal assaults.

There were, however, other avenues and Packard didn't waste any time.

Morrissey's wife, or widow, Hilda, was a nice little woman but no help at all. Packard, who told her his name was Simmons and that he was a prison visitor who had visited her husband inside, talked to her for quite a while. He was sympathetic and he did his best to draw her out but either she was scared stiff of the Sibley Boys or she genuinely didn't know anything. Packard fancied the latter was in fact the case. And she was undeniably a little simple. She kept on saying, miserably, 'Bob never told me anything, Mr Simmons, it was all such a shock. I never knew a thing about what the police said he was doing. I couldn't believe it, really I couldn't.' This, Packard knew, accorded with what had come out at the trial—he had read the police evidence in back numbers of *The Times* after leaving Forbes. 'He never came to see me after he escaped, neither.'

And that was about the lot, basically. Packard, who had come ostensibly to commiserate, murmured more words of sympathy and left, but not before he had noted the truth of what Forbes had told him: this was no breadline home. Morrissey had been a bricklayer's mate, with longish spells of unemployment in between, before he had hitched himself to the Sibley Boys. The house itself was still in line with his income group as a building labourer—it was a two-up and two-down terrace job in a dreary Paddington backwater—but that was where poverty ended. The carpets were expensive, so was the colour television—and *that* hadn't been bought before Morrissey went inside, either. Mrs Morrissey wore clothes which the wives of building labourers didn't normally wear and she had one or two nice pieces of jewellery. Packard had tried to probe but the results had been frustrating. Hilda Morrissey said she drew her State benefits and her husband had had a little money put away. Pressure brought out a little more: once a month a packet 'from the insurance' reached Mrs Morrissey by post—with two hundred pounds in cash. These payments had started soon after Morrissey had gone inside and had been kept up ever since. Yes, she'd been surprised enough when a man had telephoned to tell her about the money, but he'd told her Morrissey had taken out some sort of policy, and she really hadn't understood...except that she mustn't talk about it or it would stop. She hadn't been suspicious at that? No, not really, she'd been glad enough to have it, like, and hadn't bothered her head about it no further. She peered at Packard anxiously, her stout little body trembling a little now. Was it all right, did he think? Probably, he told her, and she mustn't worry...and all he could deduce for his private rumination afterwards was that Morrissey must have had a friend he could trust; it would scarcely be a case of the Sibley Boys being generous. Strings would certainly have been attached to any generosity from that quarter.

Packard paid his second call at the Burgoyne home, which was in Balham, and here things began to look a little brighter.

In answer to his ring a small shrewish woman opened the door. 'Yes?' she said.

'Mrs Burgoyne?'

'That's me. What d'you want, mister?'

'A word with you, if I may.'

'Go on, then.' She wiped her hands on a flowered apron. 'What is it?'

Packard said, 'I don't suppose you want the neighbours to hear your business, Mrs Burgoyne.'

'Oh. Like that—is it?'

'Yes.'

She asked directly, in a hard voice, 'Is it about *Mr* Burgoyne?'

'Yes.'

'Oh,' she said again. 'All right then, you better come in, I s'pose.' She held the door wider and stood back and Packard walked past. She banged the door to behind him. 'In there,' she said. 'On the right.' The door was open and he went into a small sitting-room which, again, was nicely fitted out. Burgoyne's wife—her name as he

21

already knew was Edith—came in behind him and said 'Well?' She had her hands on her hips now and was staring at him with bright, sharp eyes, critical and suspicious eyes. 'You the police, are you, eh?'

Packard said, 'No, I'm not. Mind if I sit down?'

She shrugged. 'If you want.' She fumbled in her apron pocket and brought out a packet of cigarettes and a box of matches. She lit and inhaled and blew down her nostrils. 'If you're not the police, who are you?'

Packard went into his prison-visitor spiel. He did it convincingly. She asked, 'Know where Brett is, do you?'

'No,' he said, 'I don't. I was wondering if you did, Mrs Burgoyne.'

'That's a laugh,' she said, but there was no laughter in her face at all. 'Wouldn't be likely to let *me* know where he was, would he?'

'Why not?'

She gave him another sharp look, hesitated, then said, 'Well, stands to reason. If he came here, it wouldn't be long before the cops had him, would it?'

Packard nodded. 'True. But he wouldn't necessarily have to come here, would he? I mean, he could be in touch in other ways. A letter, or a message by a friend. Or a telephone call.'

'On a tapped phone, mister?' Her voice was shrilly sardonic. 'These days, phones is as dangerous as a visit if you ask me. Anyway, he hasn't been in touch, not by any method you want to name he hasn't.'

Packard grinned. 'Not that you'd be telling anyone even if he had, Mrs Burgoyne?'

This time she did laugh. 'I never said that, did I? It's not necessarily true, neither. Look, mister. I don't like cops, and I wouldn't help them find Brett. Not exactly help. But if a copper happens to get his hands on Brett Burgoyne it suits me. I never want to see him again, mister. Never.' She stubbed out her cigarette. Packard saw the shake in her fingers. 'Want to know why?'

'It's up to you,' Packard said.

'Sure it is, and I'm going to tell you. All the time he was inside I stood by him, went to see him regular, wrote as many letters as I was allowed to, never put a foot wrong. All right. So how does he pay me back for that?' Her voice was vicious now, her eyes as hard as diamonds and as bright, with a red, angry glint. 'It's the old story, mister. You can guess if you try hard enough.'

'Another woman?'

Edith Burgoyne laughed again. 'If you can call her that. Just a bit of a thing, twenty-one years old, and skinny like a beanpole, no figure, just like a pencil all the way up. *Twenty-one*... at his age! Don't know what she sees in him, must be like a dad, he must. Been going on a couple of years before he went inside, what's more.' She stopped and lit another cigarette, her chest rising and falling fast. 'Soon as he got sprung like, he went to her. Not to me.'

'How do you know that?'

'Stands to reason.'

'You mean you don't know it as a fact?'

'I know it all right. In here.' She pressed a hand to her breast. 'Oh—all right, then. Not for what you'd call a fact, no.'

'I see. I don't remember this coming out at the trial?'

'It didn't,' she said. 'Because I didn't know it then. Tell you something else, too: I never have said nothing to the coppers.'

'Why not?'

24

She said shrilly, 'I told you, didn't I? I'm not helping them, not on principle I'm not. They can dig their own dirt, thank you very much!'

'When did you get to hear, Mrs Burgoyne?'

She said, 'Not till after he was sprung.'

Packard nodded and asked, 'Who is this girl?'

'I don't know,' she answered flatly. 'I don't know her name nor where she lived—or where she is now, which'll be with my husband, like I said.'

'How did you know what she looked like, then?'

'Because of how I got to know. A photograph came, by post. Anonymous—of course! With full information that tallied —so I knew it wasn't just some kind friend's idea of a funny joke. Times in the past when he'd been away from home...he used to go away a lot, see, abroad mostly I think, though he never would say. Away more often than home, he was. Then there were things in the letter, other things...things he used to say to me private like that no one else could know about—what I'd thought he wouldn't say to anyone *but* me, know what I mean?

Oh, it made sense,' she said bitterly. 'I'm convinced, don't worry!'

Packard asked, 'Have you still got that photograph?'

'Yes,' she said, 'I've got it all right. Don't ask me why I ever kept it, but I did. I've lost the letter, not that I'd ever have wanted to read that again.'

'May I see the photograph?'

'If you want to,' she said, and there was a sneer in her voice. 'It's not pornographic if that's what you're after.' She opened a drawer in a sideboard and raked around a mass of letters and other photographs and old shopping lists and after a while she said, 'Here you are then,' and passed the photograph to Packard.

It was a snap, taken of Burgoyne and his girl-friend on some beach or other with a pier in the background. It could have been Southend. Mrs Burgoyne, when he asked her, didn't know. Again Packard noted the Italianish look. The girl had long fair hair that curled attractively up beneath her chin. She was tall and thin, if not as thin as a natural bitterness had made Burgoyne's wife describe her, and she was wearing a very brief bikini with the pants slung very low on her hips. She was a good-looker and she would stand right out in a crowd. There was an appealing impudence in her expression and she had big eyes and a (no doubt misleading) innocence in her face. She was clearly a much more desirable bedmate than Edith Burgoyne had ever been...

Packard looked up and caught the woman's expression before she could alter it. There was no real misery there, no sense of loss, just bitterness and something else: a kind of salaciousness, almost as though her imagination was working overtime on what the girl and her husband would be doing at night...and a spiteful anger mixed in with it all, a desire to hurt.

Casually Packard said, 'I don't suppose you'll mind if I hang on to this for a while? You'll get it back later.'

She looked at him suspiciously. 'What d'you want it for? What are you going to do with it? Look, have I bin talking to a——cop all this time after all?'

Packard said, 'I give you my word, Mrs Burgoyne, I'm not a cop. Cross my heart. All I want is—to talk to your husband. With this photograph, I just might be able to identify the girl, you never know. If I can find her, maybe I'll find him.'

'And then?'

Packard said carefully, 'I've a few things to ask him. I'll be honest and say it could lead to his arrest again, indirectly. Even though I'm not the police.'

'And back into prison?'

'Of course. I'm sorry, but—'

'You don't need to be sorry. I told you. He's nothing to me, nothing at all.'

'But he still provides you with money.' Packard looked round at the well-furnished room that had obviously been redecorated with the best materials not so long ago. 'Does that come from 'the insurance,' by the way?'

Her eyes narrowed. 'What do you mean, mister?'

'Two hundred quid a month...or thereabouts?'

'Look,' she said, 'Not a chance. I work, don't I?'

'Do you?'

She almost spat. 'Yes. I'm a cook, up at the hospital. Been off a day or two with my chest. That keeps me all right.'

'I didn't think the National Health Service paid all that well.'

'It keeps me,' she repeated. 'I don't need Brett's dirty money.'

28

'Didn't he leave you with any, when he went inside?'

'That's my business. You're not the police. You said so.'

'That's very true,' Packard said.

After that he waited, saying nothing. Experience had taught him that most people, faced with silence, felt an urge to speak themselves. Mrs Burgoyne evidently failed to feel that urge, however, for he got no more out of her. Except for the photograph.

The Burgoyne home was in much the same sort of street as Morrissey's except that the lower fronts had bow windows of heavy, ugly brick and tiny squares of largely concreted gardens. In the vicinity were several handily situated pubs. Packard went into all of them within the radius of what might have been considered Burgoyne's former 'local'. He chatted casually with the bar custodians and after he had got them in the right frame of mind he produced the photograph. But no one remembered having seen the girl, nor Brett Burgoyne either. At least, not in the bar. One woman had known Burgoyne by sight and that was all. Evidently he had not been a drinker, at any rate not locally, and the girl didn't seem to have been local either. Maybe Burgoyne had believed in the old adage about not fouling your own doorstep.

Packard garaged the Ferrari beneath his flat in Chevenix Mews and, because he meant to do a little drinking by way of relaxation, took a taxi to Felicity Teal's address in South Kensington.

'Punctual for once,' the girl said, smiling into his eyes. She was looking extremely attractive and was using a sexy scent. She asked, 'Where are we going?'

'There's a rather nice Greek place in the King's Road. That do?'

'That'll do fine,' she said. She reached up and pulled his head down towards her lips and kissed him on the mouth. He felt the instant reaction as her body pressed against his. Gently he took her arms and lifted them away. He followed her out of the flat and found another taxi and soon they were sitting at a secluded table in a corner, under shaded light that made Felicity even more desirable. Felicity Teal was officially 'safe' security-wise and Packard was able to talk to her about his recent investigations. And he showed her the photograph. She studied it and said, 'Well, she's good-looking all right. Sexy. But nice with it, I'd say. I think.'

'And I think I'd probably agree. But just now it's not her virtues or otherwise that interest me.' He tapped the photograph. 'I want an identification. Is that Southend Pier?'

'Not Southend,' she said. 'It doesn't look long enough, unless it's the camera angle. What made you think it was Southend?'

He shrugged. 'Just because I *did* think it looked long enough and I associate length with Southend Pier. But then I'm not really well up on piers and proms and all that sort of thing.'

'And you think I am?' she asked with a glint of amusement in her eyes.

'Well, it was just a chance, that's all.'

'Perhaps the chance has paid off. I think I can give you your identification, as it happens, James.' She looked again at the snap, frowning a little. 'I may be wrong, but I'm pretty sure that's Bognor Regis. It's sort of...blank at the sea end, if you follow. And it looks sort of unfinished, doesn't it. Bognor Pier looks rather like that—since they had the fire. Or it did. I don't know if they've done any re-building

31

since I was there last.'

Packard said, 'Thanks a lot, Felicity. You've earned this expensive meal I'm buying you. If you're right, that is.'

She was still frowning as she asked, 'Do you really mean to go to Bognor, just on the chance you might find that girl? They were probably only there on holiday. If it *is* Bognor to start with.'

He nodded. 'I know. But it's the only lead I have and I need to use it. That girl's the one person I know of who ought to have a good line out on Brett Burgoyne.'

It was Bognor Regis all right. Packard found that out the following morning after a fast run out of London. He was pretty certain of his facts the moment he got himself into the proper visual angle and compared the snap with the reality. And after that he had a hard day's trudge. He parked the Ferrari near the sea front and walked around the pubs and cafés, getting into conversations and showing the snap, just as he had done back in Balham.

He struck oil at last in a café in a narrow street off the main shopping centre. The proprietor, a stringy man in a dirty white jacket, didn't need to look for long at the snap. He wiped the back of a hand across his mouth and said, 'Yes, I know the girl all right, don't know about the bloke, not for certain that is. But that bird stood out a mile. Sexy—you know what I mean?'

'Yes,' Packard said. 'Does she come here often, then?'

'Not now,' the man told him, 'but she used to not so long ago. Came here for lunch most days. Then she stopped—just like that.'

Packard asked, 'How long ago would that have been?'

'Oh, I dunno...must be around a couple of months or so, I reckon.'

'I suppose you wouldn't know her name, would you?'

The man shook his head. 'No, sorry. That, I couldn't tell you.' Then he added, 'I can tell you where she worked, though, cos I seen her there too. Fangleton's. Chemist's, just around the corner. Turn right when you leave here. You probably passed it on your way.'

'Maybe I did. Well—thanks a lot for your help.' Packard, who had drunk enough coffee to last a lifetime, finished the cup and paid and left. Two minutes later he was in Fangleton's and there the trail ended in a blank, blank wall. In a back room Packard talked to the elderly chemist, who told him the girl had left two months earlier without giving notice and when he had gone round to her lodgings personally the landlady had told him, in a scandalised voice, that she had left there as well, just packed up suddenly and departed, and had given no address, no indication at all of where she was going to. Packard paid a visit to these lodgings himself but got no further information at all and even the fact that he now had the girl's name—Lois Chailey—wasn't really very much help. By this time she was most probably calling herself something else. Nevertheless, acting on an impulse—a kind of premonition it could have been, he thought later—he bought an envelope, wrote LOIS CHAILEY on the back of the snap, and mailed it off to Forbes before returning to the Ferrari. Then he drove fast and frustratedly back towards London, and it was as he was approaching a left-hand intersection on the A29 just beyond Five Oaks that a Jag that had been behind him for the last ten or so miles took the opportunity of a clear road to roar past him and half turn, right across him, for the left-hand intersection. Furiously he slammed on his brakes and wound down his window ready for a slanging match. When he saw the doors fly open and the four men scrambling out, he reached for his gun, but they were a shade too quick and before he could slide off the 'safe' of his automatic a revolver was staring him in the face and the eyes of the man holding it told him it was going to be used if it had to be. As the Jag went on, slowly now, into the side turning, one of the men, also armed, got into Packard's passenger seat and the man who was holding the gun in his face said, 'Just follow behind the Jag, Mister bloody Packard, and don't try anything funny, all right?'

Packard shrugged and did as he'd been told. In the cover of the side turning, which was little more than a country lane, the Jag stopped and Packard stopped behind it and then a gun-barrel took him hard on the temple and he went out cold.

THREE

The name over the shop-front was Adam
Fast and it had been done in gold leaf and
in Old English lettering. Shop-front was
possibly not the word the proprietor would
have used himself; the place was more
like a boutique—an antique boutique. It
was in a discreet Mayfair street and it
looked opulent. Adam Fast had nothing
in his window, ever, except just one highly
expensive object, changed periodically for
another equally rare and expensive, sitting
in state on a thick maroon carpet. Inside,
there never appeared to be any staff. Nor
were there many customers. Adam Fast
himself was a good-looking man in the
middle thirties with well-shampooed brown
hair curling round his ears. He dressed in
muted Carnaby Street style. He was a
shade too fat and puffy as a result of
too much self-indulgence, and a little too
white, but that was all. He had a good-
natured expression usually, and he smiled
often, and rarely lost his temper. Women,

however, were inclined to be wary of him and they tended also—and contrarily—to resent his obvious lack of interest in them. For the rest of it Adam Fast was very highly polished but had never quite lost a cockney accent. His real name was Albert Fishton and he had been born in Poplar, the son of a docker. These days Poplar didn't see much of Adam Fast, except when occasionally work took him down that way.

Currently he was sitting in his office behind the boutique, his puffy-backed hands clasped across a comfortable stomach, talking business with a tall thin man with dangerous eyes that narrowed to slits whenever he asked a question, a man with a bad shake in his nicotine-stained fingers.

The puffy man asked, 'Where have you taken Packard?'

'Hollies.'

'I see—good. It's better to keep him out of London.' The house called The Hollies was discreet enough; it lay well back from a minor road in thickly wooded country just south of Abinger Hammer. 'Have you...got anything out of him, Rollo?'

'Not yet. He won't utter, not anything.

He's been searched, of course, but he wasn't carrying anything that helps.'

'The boys are still trying—to make him talk, I mean?'

Rollo said impatiently, 'Of course they are, but it's beginning to look like a job for you, Adam.'

'Oh, dear, I was afraid you were going to say that.' Fast took a handkerchief out of his breast pocket and dabbed at his lips. They were full and very red in the white face. His eyes suddenly had a curious gleam in them and he looked down as if to hide it. 'Is it *really* essential, d'you think, Rollo?'

'Yes.'

Fast shifted slightly in his chair. 'Oh, very well,' he said. 'I'll try to make time.'

Rollo said, 'I'd try to make it quick if I was you. Packard'll be being looked for, won't he? I'd like to shift him soon as possible.'

'The Hollies,' Fast said disparagingly, 'is as safe as the Bank of England, and you know it.'

Rollo shrugged. 'It always has been, yes. There always has to be a first time, though.'

Fast gave him a blank look, his mouth sagging open a little way. 'Now, what do you mean by that, Rollo?'

Rollo looked at his watch and got to his feet. 'I'll have to be away,' he said casually. 'As to what I mean...when Criminal Warfare Agencies find their top man gets knocked off, they pull their fingers *right* out. Or so I reckon. And somebody *could* have spotted the cars.'

Back at The Hollies Rollo was admitted by a woman who looked like a housekeeper, a woman quietly and neatly dressed and with a figure like a board and steel-grey short hair. She asked, 'Well?'

'Well, what?'

She said impatiently, 'Will he come down?'

Rollo laughed harshly and his eyes slitted. 'Come off it, Lily. Did you ever doubt he'd come? The fat bastard can't wait. I could see it in his face. This time, he didn't even give me the spiel about his flaming sensibilities.' He peeled off his jacket and threw it across the hall, where it landed on an oak chest against a cream-painted wall. 'How's Packard?'

'Same as ever,' the woman said indifferently. 'Keeps wanting a drink.'

'So do I,' Rollo said, making for a door. 'And with that head, I don't wonder at it!'

'Your head?'

'Packards.' Rollo went across the room towards a cupboard, where he lifted out a bottle of Haig and a glass and poured himself a neat shot. It went down his throat as straight as a die. He poured another.

The woman sat down. She asked, 'When's he coming?'

'When he's ready.' Rollo went over to the woman and reached out to her but she pushed his groping hand away. 'Leave me alone,' she snapped. The hand went back and again she pushed it away and then got up and walked out of the room.

'Lousy bitch,' Rollo called after her.

Packard's head was still like a bomb that had somehow managed to burst and yet at the same time stay whole, painfully, rackingly whole. It hadn't been just that gun-barrel, he didn't know how long before; since then, he'd been having what they had called the preliminary treatment, which had consisted of fist-slams in the face

40

and on the head, repeatedly, in between rounds of seemingly endless questioning. After a while rubber hosing had replaced the bare fists. His head had rung like a bell and once or twice, he knew, he had passed right out and had come round to feel cold water on his face and head and then the treatment had gone on again.

He hadn't answered any of the questions they'd put to him and then they'd grown really angry and the hose had been used harder, but he still didn't talk. In any case, he hadn't known the answers to half the questions. For their part they had refused to answer any of his, wouldn't tell him how they had got on to him or—somewhat naturally he had to admit—where Brett Burgoyne was, or the girl, who had very likely been hooked like he had himself, not that they had given him any hint that this was so. He thanked God for the hunch that had made him mail off that snap. After a while—a long while, though again he had no idea just how long—they had called it a day and left him, with a threat of worse to come. So he lay where he was, strapped down with heavy leather straps to a bare mattress on an iron bedstead in what looked like a dressing-room, with a small dormer window, currently tight shut and with bars across. Maybe it had been a nursery once—a charming thought, that, in present circumstances—or maybe it had merely been converted recently into a prison. There was no furniture of any kind in the room, other than the bed. And he fancied, from that dormer window, that it was an attic with, presumably, a long drop down.

The future didn't look too hopeful.

Felicity Teal, of course, knew he'd gone to Bognor. That wouldn't be a hell of a lot of help. Bognor was a biggish sort of place, and even when they found the café and the chemist and the landlady—which they would, since Forbes would have got that snap and anyway Felicity also knew the direction his enquiries were to take—it still wouldn't lead them to him.

And in the meantime, escape just wasn't on at all.

He had fallen into a kind of nightmarish, exhausted sleep when the door opened again and Rollo came back in with another man, a soft, fat man with over-long hair and a good-natured expression that Packard happened to know was entirely false.

He stared at the man and said, 'Well, well, if it isn't Albert Fishton. Frankly, I didn't realise they'd let you out. Don't tell me you actually rated good conduct remission?'

Adam Fast was looking astonished, though he didn't seem especially put out. He said, 'We've never met, so far as I know.'

'But you've obviously heard about me?'

'Yes.'

'Well, I've heard of you, too. And we have a set of photographs of you in the files. Head and shoulders—full face—both profiles—nice back view. With a prison hair-cut. But in spite of that, you're unmistakable, Fishton. So's your record. Borstal, the Scrubs, the Island and the Moor—right?'

'Right,' Fast said softly and smoothly. 'Any more you know, Packard?'

'Yes. The charges. Robbery with violence, GBH, using guns against the police when resisting arrest.'

'You have the record straight,' the puffy-faced man said. He was still basically unconcerned and he had an anticipatory look about him now. 'There's one thing you've left out, though.'

'Oh? What's that?'

'Last time I went down, the judge made a few comments on my methods. It was in connection with the GBH. Scientific...that's what he said I was. Scientific.' He caught the other man's eye and nodded. 'Rightyoh, Rollo,' he said cheerfully.

'Scientific' was possibly an exaggeration, but certainly Adam Fast was more efficient at beatings-up than Rollo and the other men had been. First of all the straps were removed and Packard was held under Rollo's gun while, under orders from Fast, he stripped. Stripped, he was pushed back on the bed and strapped down again.

Adam Fast sat by his side on the mattress and lit a cigarette. He puffed smoke into Packard's eyes and said conversationally, 'Now, as you already know, there are just a few points that need clearing up and I'd much appreciate your help.' He paused. 'First, I want to know precisely why you made that trip to Bognor.'

'As you said—I'm aware of what you want to know. I'm not saying a thing, Fishton.'

'And then,' Fast went on, in no way put

44

out, 'I'll want to know what you discovered while you were there.'

'You'll be lucky.'

'And also what, if anything, you have reported back to your office. It would also be of great help to me if you'd tell me who it was that passed you the information that made you decide to visit Bognor—not that I haven't got my own ideas on that, of course. And finally, I'll want to know in detail what your organisation is doing—that is, the lines they're working along.'

Packard asked, 'In what connection, Fishton?'

'Fast is the name.' He began to look a little annoyed. 'Come now, Packard, you don't think I'm that green. I know you know I know...what's been put on your plate. And I may as well tell you here and now, no one is going to find Lois Chailey. Or Brett Burgoyne either. You won't gain anything by holding out on me, you know. There's no point in being a martyr.'

Packard said, 'Get knotted. I'm not answering any of your questions.'

'Oh, don't be so silly, of course you're going to,' Fast said amicably. He smiled and puffed at his cigarette and then moved his hand downwards and the cigarette-end lightly touched Packard's flesh where it wouldn't easily be seen afterwards. Pain shot through Packard's body like a knife-thrust and he jerked against the straps. Fast said, 'Well now, that's just for a start. Question One again: *Why did you make that trip to Bognor?*'

He was a mass of burns after a couple of hours of science—science and, on his part, silence. He just set his teeth and took it, trying to fix his mind on something else. Something nice—like taking Felicity Teal out to dinner, or the fat salary CWA were paying him to risk having to endure this sort of treatment...things like that. It helped; but it didn't dull the pain that had accumulated by the time Adam Fast tired and stopped and, looking really angry now, said, 'I'll be back. That's a promise. And next time it'll be worse unless you talk right away. That's a promise too.'

Fast and Rollo went out of the room, leaving Packard still stripped. The door was locked behind them. Packard lay and listened to their footsteps on what sounded as though it might be parquet and then the footsteps stopped and, faintly, he caught the sound of a door being banged and a couple or so minutes after that he heard a shrill scream. It was a woman's scream and somehow Packard fancied it was unlikely to come from the flat-chested housekeeper who had brought up his bread and water from time to time.

In which case it was just possible the girl Lois Chailey was also being held here.

FOUR

There were no more screams so far as Packard could hear, but it was a long time before he heard the door slam again and the footsteps coming back and then going down the stairs. He still felt convinced the girl who had screamed must be Lois Chailey. He could only hope she wouldn't have suffered in the same way as he had himself; he was a mass of disseminated pain and his head ached more than ever. And he wasn't left alone for long, either. He heard men coming back up the stairs again and his door opened and Rollo and Adam Fast came in.

47

Packard ran his tongue over his lips. He felt dehydrated, dry as an old bone. He asked, 'Who's the girl, the one who screamed?'

'You'll find out.' It was Rollo who spoke and he was slurring his words a little and there was a smell of whisky on his breath. Adam Fast stood there covering Packard with a gun. Rollo bent and started to loosen the straps that held Packard to the bed.

Packard asked, 'What now?'

The puffy man said, 'We're moving out.' He sounded displeased, as though he'd been talked into something against his will. 'We're going a long way, Packard.'

'Where to?'

Fast said, 'Like the girl—you'll find out.' That was all he would say, other than to tell Packard, when he was free of the straps, to get dressed.

Groggily, Packard stood up. He felt sick and giddy and all he wanted to do at that moment was to have his burns attended to and then have a good shot of Scotch followed by a nice long sleep. It seemed, however, that he would have to wait a while yet. In the meantime he had things to do, and without wasting

48

time he started to do one of them. He bent down to the floor to pick up his clothes, which were lying in a heap by the bed, and as he straightened he swung out with his trousers, gripping the leg-ends and using the top part as a kind of sling. Rollo yelled a warning but the trousers had already wrapped themselves around Fast's gun and Packard had landed a fist right in the man's mouth. Adam Fast went down moaning and his gun, which he was still holding, went off and sent a bullet zipping into the ceiling. Plaster spattered down from around the hole. Packard ducked and twisted, avoiding Rollo's counter-attack, and going in to give him the same as the puffy man, who was still on the ground moaning. But a moment later it was all over, because Adam Fast had collected himself enough to get a grip on Packard's ankle and he had heaved, and Packard, caught off guard from that direction, had crashed and then he had both men's weight on his guts and the back of his head was being thumped mercilessly into the floor.

When they got off him, he obeyed orders and dressed. Within five minutes they were on their way downstairs. There had been no sign of any activity around the top of the house, from the direction the screams had come from, but down in the hall Packard saw two more men, some of the party that had ambushed him on the A29, plus two women: the grey-haired housekeeper, and a girl.

The girl—Lois Chailey. He recognised her from the photograph immediately. She was certainly pretty, and sexy enough for anybody, but just now she wasn't looking her best. Her face was tight and strained and there were deep, dark rings beneath her eyes and she was shuddering as though she had a high fever. Packard almost forgot his own body-pain in a surge of disgusted fury against Adam Fast and Rollo and the Sibley Boys—whom this lot must be part of—in general. The girl, in spite of her association with Brett Burgoyne, who would scarcely be any mum's ambition for a daughter, looked nice. She didn't seem the sort that would associate with crime and the chances were that she'd had no idea, originally at any rate, what sort of world Brett Burgoyne was part of. So all this would have come doubly hard and she would be in a pretty poor way psychologically.

Rollo said, 'Okay, Packard, move. You've

seen girls before, haven't you?' The puffy man moved past them and stood by the front door, holding his gun with one hand and a handkerchief to his bloody mouth with the other. His eyes were killing Packard every inch of the way. Rollo said, 'Go towards the door. There's a car outside. Get in the back and don't try any more tricks, all right?'

Packard shrugged and went out through the front door. The fourth man of the party was sitting in the driver's seat, all ready to go. This time it wasn't the Jag; it was a Van Den Plas Princess. The man in the front was dressed like a conventional chauffeur and when the grey-haired woman took her place beside him she completed the picture nicely of a well-to-do *ménage* on the move with the boss servants up front. When Packard was in he was joined by the girl and by Rollo and the two men who had been waiting in the hall. Rollo sat himself between Packard and Lois Chailey while the two other men sat watchfully on the let-down backward-facing seats. There were no guns visible but there were bulges around beneath the jackets to indicate the shoulder-holsters.

The Princess started up and moved

51

down a gravelled drive. Packard asked, 'What about Fishton?'

Rollo said, 'Mr Fast isn't coming.'

'I've gathered that much. Is he staying in the house, or going somewhere else?'

'Shut up.' After that no one spoke as the Princess turned out of the drive towards Abinger Hammer. No one spoke until a little later on Lois Chailey began sobbing and one of the men on the let-down seats said, 'Stop that racket, can't you?' and then, when it went on, leaned forward and slapped her hard across the face, twice. She did her best to hold it in after that. Packard felt his head would burst with the frustration of sitting there and taking it. After a while he asked again, 'Where are we going?' but all he got in answer was another order to shut up. They were travelling fast and it wasn't so very long before they had left the countryside behind them and were moving into London's outer suburbs and then into the heart of the capital to hit the Edgware Road and join the M1 at Brockley Hill. From then on the Princess hugged the fast lane and they made no stops at any of the service areas *en route* and at Kirkby-in-Ashfield in Derbyshire, as it was growing dusk, they turned off the motorway and headed west for Alfreton where they turned onto the A61 for the north. When they had passed Sheffield and it was full dark Rollo spoke through an intercom to the driver and the Princess slowed and a little later pulled off the road into a lay-by. One of the men facing Packard climbed out stiffly and ferreted around in the boot and came back with a picnic basket and they ate sandwiches and drank coffee and then, after switching drivers, drove on again. They drove right through the night and after another stop for breakfast somewhere beyond the Scottish border they drove right through the next day as well, or most of it, through largely breathtaking glen and highland scenery that at any other time Packard would have appreciated to the full; and they ended up at a long, low-built house on the shores of Loch Torridon in Ross.

'It's beautiful, all right,' Rollo said. There was a high moon that night, and it was casting silver over the Shieldaig Forest behind the house, not that Packard could see that. Rollo, looking out from the barred window of the room where Packard had been locked, sounded quite romantic, a fact that Packard found surprising, though he knew well enough that men like Rollo often had a softer side—especially when they were full of Scotch whisky. 'Lovely. One of my grandmothers was Scottish. Came from Wester Ross, 'smatter of fact.'

'Really?'

'Yes.' Rollo burped. 'The surroundings won't be concerning you for long, though.'

'Oh? We're getting on the move again, are we?'

'You are,' Rollo said with a nasty laugh. 'Not so far this time, though. Least...that depends how you look at it.'

'I don't follow?'

Rollo swung round from the window and moved towards the bed. As in the South of England, Packard was strapped down tight and hard. Rollo's gaze lingered on him for a while then the man went on, 'I may as well tell you now. You're going to be given another chance to talk and if you don't—'

'I've already said, I don't know anything. Not beyond what I've told you.' On the way up, seeing the girl was there anyway, he'd told Rollo he had been looking for her—nothing could be lost by that admission now—and that Lois Chailey had been the sole reason for his visit to Bognor. But clearly none of the mob believed that this was the sum total of what he could tell them.

Rollo repeated this disbelief, jeeringly. 'It's up to you,' he said. 'If you talk—okay. If you don't...well, we have orders to knock you off. Mr Fast doesn't want you around. For one thing, you know a little too much now, don't you? If you were to get away—or if you were to be found—'

Packard said, 'Bodies can be found too, you know.'

'Sure I know, but they can't talk, and anyway yours isn't ever going to be found. Nor the girl's.'

'You mean to kill her too?'

Rollo said, as though speaking to a lunatic, 'Of course we do. She knows as much as you.'

'You mean, since you got hold of her?'

'Sure—and about other things too. From her boyfriend. And you know who I mean.' Suddenly Rollo checked himself, scowled and muttered something under his breath and then banged out of the room, locking the door behind him.

Packard had a restless night, wondering about Lois Chailey, worrying about the next move. There was no way out of this that he could see. He hadn't a hope of getting away and he didn't doubt for a moment that Rollo was dead serious and would carry out his threat. There was no curtain across that barred window and he watched the moon making shadows on the walls of the room, was still watching when the moon gave way to the dawn's light. As the sun began sending its beams into the room, and with them a little welcome warmth, Rollo and one of the other men, whom Packard had now learned was called Bearsted, came into the room.

'You're getting up,' Rollo said. History was repeating itself. The man Bearsted bent and unfastened the straps and Rollo, taking no chances this time, kept the whole operation closely covered with a sub-machine-gun cradled like a baby in his arms.

'No breakfast?' Packard asked.

'Why waste good food?'

'Oh—I see. It's like that, is it?'

'Very much so. And don't let's linger.'

'Would you mind telling me,' Packard asked evenly, 'how the knocking-off is to be done?'

'I'll do that for you,' Rollo said. He looked as though he had a stinking hangover. 'A few miles north from here, there's a stream. It's a very fast flowing stream and it's deep too. It starts from one of the smaller lochs in the Shieldaig Forest and about five miles from the source it takes a dive and goes underground. No one knows for certain just where it runs to, but the theory is, there's some sort of deep cavern right below the forest. Anyway, from time to time people have fallen in that stream and they've never been heard of again. No bodies have ever been recovered, and I guess that must mean there's no exit to the sea. That's where you and the girl are going.'

'Nice,' Packard said.

'Yes.' Rollo added, looking reflectively out of the window as he had done the night before, 'Matter of fact, I first heard about it from my old granny in Wester Ross. An uncle of hers, a gillie, had a skinful one day and went in. He was one of those that was never seen again.'

FIVE

This time there was no car ride. The trip was across country. Under any other circumstances it would have been a nice, healthy walk, just the thing to shake the liver up before tramping back to a substantial Scottish breakfast. A light mist hung through the trees and filled the clearings but the air was keen enough and after a while the mist lifted. The trees came out of their ghostly mantle and the contours of the country began to emerge. A man Packard hadn't seen until this morning was leading the way; he was a Scot, no doubt a local who knew his terrain. Behind him was the girl, then one of the Sibley mob holding a gun, then Packard, then Rollo who was also well armed and very watchful. Behind again, and keeping a kind of general rear-guard in being were two more of the thugs, the men who had been in the backward-facing seats in the Princess.

As the mist cleared Rollo called out, 'Not far now, is it?'

'A wee while yet,' the man in front answered.

Rollo grunted; the walk didn't seem to be doing him the good it should be, and he wasn't shod for this kind of territory either, Packard had noted. Packard asked, 'Where are you lot going, after you get back to the house?'

'Where d'you think?' Rollo gave a hard laugh. 'Back to the Smoke, that's where! Catch me hanging around up this way.'

'You don't like the open-air life?'

'No.'

'In spite of granny from Wester Ross?'

Rollo said belligerently, 'You leave my family out of this.'

'It was you who brought her in in the first place,' Packard pointed out, 'and seeing it was her information that put you on to the underground stream, I have a certain interest in the old lady. It's only natural, you must agree.'

'You shut your trap,' Rollo said viciously. He was breathing hard now and he let out a long sigh of relief when their guide looked over his shoulder and said, 'The stream's away over the rising ground ahead—d'ye see?' The man pointed to a tree-capped slope a few hundred yards away. 'We just

59

drop down to it...it's just as far as you can see now.'

They came up the slight slope and then down the other side. Packard could hear the fast-moving water ahead, though he couldn't yet see the stream itself. It was evidently down in a gully. A few moments later he picked out the dark slash of that gully, a line that broke open the ground between the tall Scots firs.

'There she is,' the guide said.

Packard felt Rollo closing in behind him and ahead he saw the other man push the snout of his gun right into Lois Chailey's back. There was just no hope, no chance at all of any break-out. The moment he made a move both those guns would fire and that would be that. The Sibley Boys, with a view to even so remote a possibility as the bodies being found one day, wouldn't want to plant the evidence of murder, naturally, but that would have to take second place in their priorities and the time hadn't yet come for the risk to be taken.

They went on down the slope towards the gully. It was pretty steep and they had to lean backwards to keep their footing. The ground was slippery, wet from dew and mist. The water-sounds increased but still they couldn't see the stream itself. They couldn't see it until they were almost on top of it, standing on a high, sheer bank above the leaping, racing turbulence some fifteen feet below.

On the brink, Packard looked down.

Once in that, there wouldn't be a hope in hell of getting out. The sides were smooth as glass, there were no protuberances that he could see. The speed of the flow would never give a man time to dig his fingers into the bank and get any sort of hold.

This had very much the look of the end of the road and it was obvious the Sibley Boys had precisely the same view. Rollo said, 'Right, Packard, that's it. You first.' He nodded once and all the men closed in around Packard. Rollo himself transferred his gun to cover the girl. Packard lowered his head and charged the nearest man in the guts. The man went down winded but it was a useless gesture on Packard's part. A heavy body landed on his back and someone else's boot took him in the mouth and when the man on his back got off another boot kicked him viciously in the stomach and he started the long drop as he rolled over the edge. He hit the water, went down, came up again gasping, saw briefly that he was already a long way from the group staring down from the bank and saw Lois Chailey being lifted bodily and thrown. After that all his attention was concentrated on a desperate fight against the rushing water that was carrying him along as though he were a cork. Moments later he saw what looked like a blank wall ahead, or like a bridge with floodwater flowing almost to the top of its arch, and he realised this was where the stream took its underground plunge.

He swept nearer, fast.

He saw there was going to be something like a foot clearance for his body and in the second before he came below the overhang he reached upward with both arms. He managed to get a grip. The water tugged at his clothing as if anxious to hurry him away, but he held on desperately to the crumbling earth and a moment later he felt the impact of the girl's body as it struck his head and shoulders. The flow of the water held her jack-knifed around his neck as he scrabbled at the overhang.

Panting and gasping now, he said, 'Try to get a grip of your own if you can,' but as he said it he became aware of the men racing along the bank and spreading out along the overhang above him. One of them reached down with a long branch and, dodging his groping fingers, broke away the earth where he was trying to get a grip. He slid down and the rush of the water took him and the girl and swirled them away helplessly into pitch blackness filled with the roar of the water and a distant dull booming noise.

In London all the stops had been pulled out by Forbes, working from the Throgmorton Street office and his cover as a stockbroker. But there had been no results at all. All Forbes could find were dead ends. Felicity Teal, who was worried stiff, had naturally put Forbes on the Bognor trail; but Bognor had produced nothing at all beyond the bare facts of Packard's more or less abortive calls. The name Lois Chailey scribbled on the back of the photograph that Packard had mailed to London before leaving Bognor hadn't helped either. It led precisely nowhere, evading all the checks that could be put on it. This wasn't particularly surprising, of course, since as Packard had realised himself, the girl could have been using an alias. But it wasn't particularly helpful either.

And soon after Packard and Lois Chailey had vanished on that fast-flowing water so far to the north, an urgent telephone call reached Forbes at his home address, a call from the Home Office to say that an attempt had been made to spring a man from the Isle of Wight's Parkhurst Prison and had failed because the man himself hadn't been co-operative. Which, on the face of it, was strange. And the man concerned had been one of those sentenced for the big-time robbery at Veldcamp, Beerman and Maclaren's Hatton Garden premises.

SIX

By now Packard had got an arm around the girl. He was keeping her head above water as they were swept on towards that booming noise ahead. There was air in this underground water-tunnel but it was stale and foetid and dank. It was pitch dark except for the dwindling area of daylight

64

behind them but Packard had reached up and felt the roof no more than a foot above their rushing bodies.

He had no idea now how far in they were from the underground entry; but the booming was getting closer every second and soon, over the hollow sound of that boom, he could hear the roar and splash of dropping water. He braced himself for the end. There could be no hope now; there was little point even in prolonging the business, yet his basic instinct for self-preservation had made him strike out for the side of the tunnel where the water-flow would be a shade less swift than in the middle. After a while he found he could slow their onrush a little more by digging into the side with his feet. And a moment after that something hard but apparently pliant whipped across his face. Then another. At first he didn't realise what this could mean but when the same thing happened yet again he ticked over, made a wild grab upwards with his free hand, found nothing, went on grabbing, and at last got a grip on a thin, slimy but tough protuberance: the root of a tree growing down into the waterway.

It was a breathing-space and it could be

a lifeline. He held on desperately against the tug of the stream.

Wonderingly the girl said, 'We've stopped!'

'We have,' Packard said and then put into his voice all the hope and encouragement he could muster. 'We're going to get out of this—if we don't give in! Can you hang on?'

'I guess I can a bit,' she said, and he admired her guts. 'Just tell me what to do.'

He said, 'For the time being I'm going to hang on to this root and try to gouge out a foothold in the side of the tunnel. I want you to hold on to me but move a little way back against the flow and dig out another foothold, about level with my body—just above the waterline. All right?'

'All right,' she said. Her voice was shaky but there was spirit and determination in it just the same. 'I'll do my best anyway...'

Packard got to work right away and felt the movement of the girl's body against his own as she did the same. When he had dug out a good enough cavity he brought his knee up, waited till Lois Chailey was ready also, then manoeuvred a foot into the hole.

It held. So did the girl's. They pushed

their bodies back against the current. Groping around, Packard felt for the cavity Lois Chailey had made, got his own foot in that while she clung to him, then let go the tree root. The foothold held them both, at least until Packard was able to get a grip on another root. That grip obtained, they repeated the manoeuvre again and again—until they ran out of roots.

'So what do we do now?' Lois Chailey asked. The hope had gone out of her voice this time.

Packard said, 'We just go on making footholds, that's all.' He tried to make it sound easy, as though success was merely a matter of time and patience, but he realised he was a pretty poor competitor for the insidious drag of the water and the noise from the subterranean falls that still beat against their ears as wickedly as ever. The foul air wasn't helping, either. It wasn't giving them the energy and vigour they were going to need for a long, long time yet. 'We'll have to manage without the hand-hold and make sure each hole we dig for our feet is deep enough to take the weight on its own. Don't worry—we're making progress and I've a strong feeling we're going to get out all right.'

The feeling vanished when on the first post-root foot-hole he missed out and was dragged back by the current. Lois Chailey, clinging to him hard, was drawn along with him. But once again he caught a root as he went past and patiently they began the process all over again. This time they got safely past the last of the tree-roots and foot by foot they dragged themselves along against the onrush. Their hands were sore and bruised and scratched, bleeding freely; every bone, every muscle in their bodies ached appallingly and they found their breath, after a time, hard to catch. But they struggled on and just as Packard felt the girl couldn't take any more he had the luck to strike another root and they hung on there for a full ten minutes—encouraged now by the fact that the pinpoint of light at the tunnel entry had grown very noticeably larger.

Rested, they moved on again.

Using their system of footholds they had struggled clear and then up that appallingly sheer bank and on to the lip of the overhang and from there to safe ground in the shelter of the firs.

They lay there, panting, exhausted.

The girl's face was a dead white and she was right out now, lying in an abandoned position, arms flung out and the flimsy material of her dress badly torn but clinging tightly, revealingly, to her breasts. Packard gave her all the time she needed, though he was feverishly impatient to be away. There was a lot to be done and a long way to go and the girl had to talk. But at the moment it was impossible. He just had to wait. He held her in his arms, giving her what body-warmth he could. She didn't come round for another half-hour and when she did, she began crying, not loudly or demonstratively but with shuddering sobs that racked her body. It was sheer reaction, Packard realised. The nightmare, in ending, had really caught up with her and all she had suppressed earlier was coming out now. Again he could do nothing but wait and do what he could to comfort her, to reassure her.

It was some while before she was fit to go on and when he thought she was ready he got to his feet and reached down and pulled her up. He said, 'They'll never believe we could have got out of that lot. We're written off the books by now—dead, smashed, unfindable and forgotten. That gives us a nice start.'

She asked unsteadily, 'Where do we go, then?'

'Back to the house. Rollo will probably have gone south by now—from what he said, I gathered he didn't intend to linger. The others may or may not have gone with him. In any case, that house ought to have a few clues that could be useful if we can find them.'

She shivered; the air was still keen though the sun was overhead now, and a light wind bit through what was left of her damp clothing. 'You going back there now?' she asked. 'Or waiting till dark?'

He said, 'Time could be running out for Brett Burgoyne, I know, but we mustn't throw away our advantages. We'll move on till we have the house in view, then lie up in cover till after dark.' They were moving through the trees already, in the direction Packard hoped would take them to the house by Loch Torridon. 'Meanwhile, Miss Chailey, you'd better tell me all you know about the set-up. Including Burgoyne.'

She nodded and said, 'Of course I will, if you're on my side.'

'If I hadn't been,' he told her, smiling,

'I doubt if I'd have pulled you out of that stream!'

'Unless you'd wanted to get something out of me,' she said.

'Well, I do, come to that. But it's all in your own interests, and Burgoyne's. Currently I can't prove what I'm telling you, but I'm here to make sure the boyfriend doesn't get the chop. You can confirm that for yourself the moment we hit London—or sooner, by telephone. In the meantime, you'll just have to trust me.'

She looked at him critically for a while then said, 'Well, okay. I do know you're working on the strictly right side of the law because those shysters told me so. But what I don't know is, what you mean to do to Brett.' She added, 'I'm not telling you anything that's going to hurt Brett.'

'I've told you I'm here to stop him going over the edge. That's absolutely genuine. But at the same time I'm not making any promises that as a result of what I do, the police won't re-arrest him. He's an escapee and that's that. Also he's a properly sentenced con, Miss Chailey. But believe you me, if he *is* put back inside, he's going to be a damn sight safer there

71

than if he's left to the Sibley Boys and Adam Fast, as he calls himself these days, in particular. And I want you to keep on bearing that in mind.'

She shivered again and after a moment said slowly, 'That does make sense, I know it. Because I know the Sibley Boys...'

'Right,' Packard said briskly. 'Let's have all you know.'

She said, 'That's easy enough. I don't know anything about what you want to know. I mean, I don't know where Brett is, and that's what you want to know, isn't it?'

'Yes,' he said, 'it is, but just try to think of anything that could help. And you're not holding back on me, I hope—about Burgoyne's whereabouts?'

She shook her head. 'No, I'm not, honest. And if I had known, Rollo or Adam would have got it out of me, so it's just as well I didn't. Which is maybe why Brett never contacted me after he was sprung.'

'He didn't?'

'Never at all.'

'Nor his wife either,' Packard said casually. He looked into her mud-streaked face. 'You knew he had a wife, of course?'

'Of course,' she said indifferently. 'It may surprise you, but Brett was always honest with me. I knew all about *her*. He couldn't stand her guts, he told me. He and I...we were just like that.' She held out her first and second fingers, very close. She had nice hands, he noticed, even though they were in bad shape just now. 'I love him,' she added simply and sincerely. She seemed quite unaware of any incongruity in the age-gap. 'I don't want anything to...happen to him.'

'Well, we'll try not to let it. Now. Try to think of anything that'll help. For instance, what about Brett's share of the diamonds?'

She gave him a quick sideways look as they went on through the close-growing firs. 'You know about that, then?'

'Of course I do.'

'I don't mean the robbery itself,' she said impatiently. 'I mean, that Brett managed to carve out his share and hide it away.'

He said, 'Yes, I knew that. Morrissey too.'

'Morrissey?'

'It's not going to help you, to act green,' he said. 'Morrisey's dead. He was found in a bust crate in Shoreham docks.' He could see she knew that, too. The rough-house mob would have told her whose that body had been, by way of encouragement to talk. She would have seen herself ending up that way... Packard said, 'But don't let's worry about Morrissey for now. Brett's more important—isn't he, Miss Chailey?'

She said, 'You can call me Lois if you like. I guess you've seen enough to call us intimate! And yes, Brett's much more important, believe me.' She paused then went on, 'Okay, so Brett's got his share hidden away. *I* don't know where it is.'

'You're telling me the truth, I hope, Lois?'

'Yes,' she said. 'I am. But like you I can't prove anything, so *you'll* have to trust *me*. So now it's mutual, all right?'

He grinned. 'All right. Do I gather, then, that the Sibley Boys still don't know where that loot is?'

'Dead right, they don't! Not what Brett got away with.'

There was something in her tone that made him ask, 'What d'you mean by that? That was what we were talking about anyway, wasn't it?'

She said, 'Yes. But as a matter of fact...I overheard some of them talking one time, and I got the idea they have some of their share of the diamonds stowed away somewhere in the house—the one up here.'

'Is that so?' Packard asked softly. 'Well, well! You don't know where, I suppose?'

'No,' she said, 'I don't, they didn't say anything about that and I may have got it wrong anyway. I can't even really remember what they were saying, it was just a—a kind of impression I think. I wasn't feeling too good.'

'That, I can understand.' They walked on. 'Now, Lois: what else do you know...anything at all might help?'

She frowned and said, 'Well, there's just one thing really. I don't know if it'll be any use. It's something Brett let out once—he didn't mean to, and he didn't so much let it out as...well, it was my fault, I got anxious.' She stopped.

'You're not making much sense,' Packard said, cursing as a branch caught his face.

'Sorry. Well, he had some business to do in Mayfair before he was arrested—some while back, this is, you see.' She paused. 'It was something he had to do on three or four different occasions, go and see

75

a man, he said when I asked, about some insurance. He used to leave me in Shepherd's—you know? with a drink. One day I followed him. He went into a shop in Darnton Street, that's not far from Shepherd Market. It was an antique shop. I didn't see the link with insurance. Not then anyway.'

'So?'

'Well,' she said, frowning rather attractively, 'here's the interesting thing. Maybe. The name over the shop was Adam Fast.'

'*Was* it indeed?'

'Yes, it was. And sort of looking back, you see...I think the insurance Brett was fixing up could have been an escape plan for if he got caught by the cops—which of course he did.'

Packard whistled. 'You know, you may have something there! The Sibley Boys do the job and Albert Fishton, alias Adam Fast, runs the escape organisation. Antique shops are quite nice cover!' He paused. 'Lois, tell me this: does the mob know you know this?'

She shook her head. 'I'm pretty sure they don't, or there'd have been some talk of it while they were asking me questions. Even Brett didn't know I'd seen him go

76

in. I didn't wait, I went right back to Shepherd's and he found me there when he came back. And I never let on during that questioning.' She laughed, a little shakily. 'I'm not saying I wouldn't have done if I'd seen any use in it...I kind of like being alive...but I thought it would only make matters worse if anything, so I just didn't.'

'Good girl,' he said softly. 'And thanks a lot for the information. It looks as though we have a line on Mr Albert Fishton after all!'

They had kept more or less on course and a little over two hours later they had a view of the house away to their right. Packard moved for cover from where he could watch the house and they remained concealed throughout the day, seeing no movement, and after dark they headed for the house under a clouded sky that looked full of rain. There was wind in the offing, too, and no moon. They made it soon after midnight and as they came clear of the trees they saw the big dark bulk of the building looming as a blacker shadow in the surrounding night with not a flicker of light from the windows to break it.

Somewhere ahead of them an owl hooted mournfully and Lois moved closer to Packard. Irreverently he thought this was like a conventional ghost hunt, even down to that owl. All the same, he felt more than naked without his gun.

SEVEN

They came round the back of the building, as quietly as they could, and came upon old stables converted into garages in a concreted yard. These garages were all locked. They crossed the yard to a heavily-built back door flanked by semi-basement windows. That door would never yield to anything short of high explosive; Packard jumped down into a narrow area behind a deep stone-faced embankment and examined one of the windows, trying to locate the catches and see what was beyond the window. After a while he pulled himself up again and said, 'This could be a way in, but before I try it I'm going to take a look right round the outside of the house.'

The girl nodded without speaking and kept close to him as he made his way around. The place was as quiet as the grave and still there was no light anywhere. And the chances were, in a house of this size and character, that the kitchen quarters would be pretty isolated from the bedrooms.

It was worth a chance. He put a hand on Lois Chailey's arm. 'We'll go back to that window,' he said. 'We're going in.' He led the way back around the house.

She asked, 'How do we get in?'

'I'll need to break a pane of glass and reach through to the catch. There's a couple of thumb-screws, too, but I think I'll be able to reach all right.'

'What about the noise?' Her voice was anxious, scared—and no wonder, he thought. The last thing she would want would be to get Rollo's hands on her again...He said, 'The panes aren't all that big and I don't believe anyone'll hear us, Lois. But I'll take what precautions I can.' He stopped near an over-grown flower-bed and bent down to feel the earth. 'This is nice and damp,' he said. 'It ought to help a little.' He pulled off his jacket and laid it out flat on the ground.

He gathered handfuls of the clinging earth and put them on the jacket and when he had enough he picked it up like a sack. 'Come on,' he said.

Reaching the window again he jumped down into the slit-like area and reached up to give Lois Chailey a hand. When she was down he took another look at the window, selecting the pane that he would use. He plasterd this with the thick, moist earth which he then held more or less in place with the jacket, pressing it hard against the glass. 'It's rough enough,' he said, 'but it's the best I can do and it should stop some of the glass falling through.' He bunched his fist and banged it smartly against the tweed jacket. he did this twice and on the second blow there was a sound of smashing as some of the broken glass parted company with the mud and fell onto a stone floor. Packard pulled the jacket away and reached in, after carefully removing the jags of glass still clinging to the frame, and pushed back the catch. Reaching farther in he released the thumb-screws, one of them on either side of the catch.

Then, gently, he eased the window up. It was stiff and it creaked and he had to take it slow but within ten minutes of starting the operation they were both inside and Packard was examining what was evidently a pantry. Or had been once. Now, in spite of the darkness, which was pretty total in here, he could sense that it had been unused for a long time. It smelt of damp and decay and cobwebs draped themselves across his hands and face as he moved. Starting with the remainder of the basement they went right through the house and found no one, no occupants at all. Packard said at last, 'It seems we have the place to ourselves, Lois. Now we'll need to check through again to see if they've left anything interesting hidden...it's going to take time, but it has to be one hundred per cent.'

It was one hundred per cent, or as near as Packard could make it, though the real work had to wait till daylight. Packard was efficient at this sort of thing, and experienced too. But the check didn't yield a thing. No leads, no loot. They didn't finish the job until well on into the morning; the house was big and rambling and even though most of it was empty and bare of furnishings there were still any number of possible hiding-places that had to be pulled apart—cellars, storerooms, lavatory cisterns where diamonds could be hidden; and panelling and staircases had to be gone over thoroughly against any possibility of secret stowages.

'Melodramatic,' Packard said, 'but that's the way things go even in the computer age. Even outfits like the Sibley Boys often find the old methods are still the best.'

Later on, he used the telephone, which was still connected, and called the local police. Within half an hour a startled constable had driven up with a sergeant. Packard explained, told them to take him to the nearest police station and call Forbes from there. This was done; Forbes was out but Felicity, overjoyed to hear Packard was okay after all, satisfied the law. The constable said, 'You'll be needing a meal and some sleep. The wife'll be glad to fix you up, sir.'

'It's very kind of her,' Packard said, 'and we could do with something to eat. But the sleep'll have to wait. I'd like you to fix me a self-drive car for a long trip south—with the minimum of publicity and any name used but my own. We're both dead, remember, and I'd like it to go on looking that way for as long as possible. So among other things, you see, public transport of any kind at all is right out for the time being.'

Lois shared the driving and when they reached his flat late the following night he gave the girl a bed. During the long run south he had found out she had no parents and no home. While she made some coffee in his kitchen, Packard rang Forbes's private number. Forbes sounded as though he had come out of a deep sleep but was glad to hear Packard's voice. He said, 'I have news for you. It's interesting.'

'I'm listening.'

Forbes said, 'I dare say you are, but I'm not passing it on the phone. Come round here.'

'Now?'

'Right away, James.'

'But I've got...' His voice trailed away. The phone had clicked in his ear. Irritably he put the receiver back on its rest. He went into the kitchen. 'Sorry, Lois,' he said, 'but I have to go out.'

She looked at him with a faintly scared expression. 'In the middle of the night?'

'It's been done before,' he said. 'I work for a pretty demanding sort of boss. Don't worry, though. Just go to bed and catch up on some sleep, that's all.'

She asked, 'I'll be all right, won't I? I mean...will anyone try to get at me?'

'I shouldn't think so for a moment,' he said, 'seeing that no one can possibly know you're here. Don't forget we're both lying waterlogged somewhere under the Shieldaig Forest. Just the same, don't answer the door if the bell does happen to ring.' He drank his coffee quickly, let himself out of the flat, got into his hired car again, and ten minutes later he was in Forbes's Edwardes Square apartment. Forbes was waiting for him with a very yellow glass of whisky and wearing an expensive, heavy silk dressing-gown over silk pyjamas. Forbes waved him to a seat and said, 'We won't waste time, James. Let's have your report first.'

Briefly, Packard gave him the whole thing, from Bognor through the house near Abinger Hammer and on to Loch Torridon. At the end of it Forbes said non-committally, 'Really we don't seem very much farther ahead, do we?'

Packard felt slightly ruffled and pointed

out, 'We know two of their bases—that's something.'

'If they use them again.'

'They probably will. They'll see no reason not to. Lois Chailey and I are dead and we never had a chance to talk to anyone before we died.'

'Well, yes.' Forbes put the tips of his fingers together and looked broodingly at Packard over the top of them. 'What the devil are we going to do with that girl? Have you any ideas, James?'

Packard said, 'I'd suggest she remains in my flat for the time being, I think. She can keep hidden, no need to go out or even go to the door.'

'If she agrees. We can't hold her otherwise.'

'I think she'll agree.'

Forbes smirked, 'It's like that, is it?'

'No,' Packard said irritably. 'It isn't, as a matter of fact. But she has nowhere else to go and she's scared. That's natural enough in the circumstances. I believe she feels safe so long as she's with me.'

'Good heavens,' Forbes said. 'Well, anyway—I do agree that might be best. If she's any sort of a target—I mean if word does get around that you're both alive and kicking after all—the fact that she's with you might hand us a lead on a plate. On the other hand, if we don't get somewhere soon, we may have to consider turning her loose on the world and putting a tail on her.'

Packard stifled a yawn. He had a strong feeling all this could have waited till morning. 'What was it you wanted to tell me, colonel?'

'Yesterday morning,' Forbes said with an enigmatic air, 'I had a call from the Home Office, as a result of which I went to Parkhurst prison for a chat with the Governor. And one of the cons.'

'Who?'

'Chris Kilroe.'

Packard looked blank. Forbes snapped, 'Pull your finger out, James. Kilroe was one of the mob that did Veldcamp, Beerman's premises.'

'Oh—yes. And what had he to say?'

'It was most interesting,' Forbes said, and paused irritatingly to take a pull at his whisky. 'It seems all arrangements had been made ahead for Kilroe among others—all the mob in fact—to be sprung if they should ever be caught. We know, of course, that Morrissey and Burgoyne were sprung successfully. The others have been waiting their turn and it so happens that Kilroe was next on the list. Everything was in hand...until at the last moment Kilroe decided he didn't want to go. The attempt was made—a helicopter lowered a rope when Kilroe was on an outside working party, you know the sort of thing—but no escapee appeared. Kilroe carried on working with the other cons. Afterwards, he asked to see the Governor. The interview was granted with alacrity and all red tape dispensed with.'

'And?'

'Kilroe said the attempt was for his benefit but he felt safer inside. He'd got the word about Morrissey, of course. Not that he was dead—that he'd been sprung. And Burgoyne. But apparently he had a very strong belief that both of those *would* be murdered. He said he would rather stay inside and come out when he was due and stay in one piece. And having admitted *that,*' Forbes said, 'he came out with a hell of a lot more. Stuff that didn't emerge at the trial—naturally, in the circumstances.'

'Well?'

Forbes brushed at his neatly clipped moustache. 'In spite of what was supposed to have come out at the time, the Sibley Boys as such were not directly concerned in that Hatton Garden robbery at all. They've pulled out of the game. And they've done that because they've found a way of participating indirectly and, taken overall, a damn sight more profitably: they're in the escape organising business itself, full-time and exclusive. And here's the really interesting thing: when they take on an account, like the Hatton Garden job, it's all fixed up and contracted before the job takes place, and the haul goes intact to the Sibley Boys, who have to approve the *modus operandi* and who always have a representative on the spot—taking part in the job itself. Now, the Sibley Boys act as fences, dispose of the stuff, take their whack, and credit the balance to each of their account customers. The split is fifty-fifty if anyone's copped within two years and the service paid for is a guaranteed escape, a false passport, and a free lift out of Britain. After two years the contract expires and in that case the Sibley Boys take only ten per cent. As you can see, they can't lose. They already hold the stakes!'

'Then why bother to do any springing?' Packard asked with a grin.

Forbes said, 'Well, if they didn't, they'll hardly stay in business, would they?'

'They wouldn't need to, with a job the size of Veldcamp, Beerman. Almost a million quid—that's more than enough to stop work on, isn't it?'

Forbes said, 'In this case there are special considerations, James. Diamonds aren't easily disposed of—not quickly, I mean. Not on this scale, anyway. They had to wait.'

'They could still have sold them off piecemeal and brought in enough to pay the rent! I don't quite get this, colonel. If they already had the haul tucked away somewhere safe, why the anxiety to get their claws on Burgoyne and why kill Morrissey to get his share?'

'Because,' Forbes said patiently, 'as I said—there are special factors this time. Morrissey and Burgoyne did in fact double-cross the outfit just as I suspected. One up to me! Somehow or other they found out where the Sibley Boys kept the loot and they knocked off their shares and stowed them away where no one has yet been able to find them. Got it?'

Packard whistled. 'Got it,' he said. 'And Chris Kilroe? Had he done the same?'

'Correct. He had. And it seems a little bird has been chirping, and as a result the Sibley Boys want Kilroe very badly indeed.'

'Uh-huh. Did he say where they'd stowed the stuff?'

Forbes shook his head. 'He didn't know that. Or if he did, he's refusing to say. In any case there's grounds for believing he may know something else: Burgoyne's whereabouts.'

Packard lifted an eyebrow. 'But, again, he's not saying?'

'No. Quite definitely not. I spoke to Kilroe myself, as a matter of fact. My impression, and the Governor agrees, is that he only spoke at all because he was in a highly nervous and emotional state. After he'd blurted out what I've told you, he began to regret it. He knows what grapevines are, and he's scared now he'll get carved up or worse when he *does* come out in the ordinary course of time. So he's not going to say any more—not to the authorities, that is, or to us. And frankly, I don't believe we have a hope in hell of finding Brett Burgoyne by the normal means open to us. I've reached that conclusion after talking to Kilroe, you

90

see. If the Sibley Boys can't find him after being double-crossed, a thing they'll be as sharp as knives on, Burgoyne must have got himself out of the country and we haven't a clue where. The world's a pretty big place to cover fast, and if the Sibley Boys do get to hear where he is, he won't last five minutes. And they *could* get to hear through Kilroe and the grapevine—if someone inside Parkhurst puts the pressure on him. One of his fellow cons, I mean.'

Packard nodded. 'Yes, that could happen. What do you suggest we do about that, then?'

Forbes smiled obscurely and said, 'I'm putting you right where I believe the chances are best for getting a fast line on Brett Burgoyne. You're going down for a full stretch, James. You're going to Parkhurst. You're going to be the "fellow con."'

Packard looked as shattered as he felt. 'Oh—am I? May I ask when, and on what charge?'

Forbes said crisply, 'Tomorrow. You can leave the details to me and the Governor and certain persons in the Home Office and the police with whom I've already reached agreement. There's obviously not time to have you arrested and charged and to go through all the tarradiddle of the court processes. So you're going straight to the island, via the cells at the Old Bailey, on a charge of sexual assault for which you've been sentenced to three years.'

'My God,' Packard said. 'Who have I raped?'

'Lois Chailey,' Forbes said with a grin. 'As Brett Burgoyne's girl-friend, that's going to put you in fast touch with Kilroe, isn't it? Like another shot of Scotch, James? It's the last you'll get for a while, I'm afraid.'

EIGHT

Nothing was said to Lois Chailey as to the reason for her move, but next morning Forbes arranged for her to live for the time being with a discreet woman, once employed by Criminal Warfare Agencies in Ipswich. She was taken there in Felicity Teal's car and after she had gone Packard slipped out quietly and took a taxi to

Northumberland Avenue. From there he walked through to New Scotland Yard and asked for a Chief Superintendent Birkin. He was in the Yard for rather over an hour talking to Birkin and other senior officers and at the end of that time he left in a police car for the Old Bailey accompanied by a detective inspector and with his jacket pulled over his head. At the Old Bailey he was hurried out of the car, still with his face covered, and guided by the detective inspector into the building and the cells beneath.

He spent some hours there and then the door of the cell was unlocked and a gaoler ordered him peremptorily out. He was escorted, with other prisoners, to a Black Maria and driven to Pentonville Prison. Here he went through the routine in the name of Henry Paul Perkins, occupation turf accountant's clerk with an address, which could be checked by any con who wanted to do so and had friends outside to do it for him, in Battersea.

Next morning he was transferred, again with other convicts, to Parkhurst.

They went down by road in a convoy of four police cars and each man was handcuffed to a prison officer. Probably, Packard thought, this means of transport had been laid on specially. He doubted if his particular crime would, on its own, merit the VIP treatment; rape was bad but it still wasn't murder or big-time espionage and it wasn't as though he was fresh from a trial that had hit the national headlines. He could presumably have travelled by train from Waterloo and then by British Rail ferry to Ryde pier, but Forbes would have had it in mind that if he had done that there was just a chance, however long a shot, that he could have been spotted by Adam Fast or Rollo or one of the others he had met just recently and when the news hit the various prisons where the Sibley Boys' protégés were incarcerated, the news that James Packard was part of a chain gang, it would look a trifle high to say the least. In the meantime Packard, doing his best to play his part, had contrived almost to think of himself as a con. Irreverently, he found himself wondering what it would have been like really to have raped Lois Chailey. He hadn't appreciated his first night in gaol and if he had been a raper he would never, never have repeated the offence, that was for sure. The indignities of the processes of imprisonment—the taking of personal particulars, the cursory but intimate medical inspection, the enforced bath, the prison-issue clothing, the lack of identity—all these had been as bad as the actual loss of freedom itself. The impersonal attitude of the prison officers had grated and despite all his years of experience of subterfuge he had been conscious of an almost overwhelming impulse to tell them all, as loudly and as clearly as he could, that he wasn't really a con, that rape was something so far removed from his mental approach to life—besides being totally unnecessary to him—that he would no more have committed such a crime than he would have murdered his mother.

Now, as the police car went fast down the A3 for Portsmouth, he found he was looking at freedom as though he had been deprived of it for the last ten years. It was a highly curious feeling. They passed through Hindhead, Haslemere, Petersfield, and came over Portsdown Hill to drop down into the city of Portsmouth and head for the Camber, Portsmouth's commercial port, where the convoy drove aboard the car ferry for the Island. Packard smelt the sea through the wound-down driver's window, heard the slop of it against the blunt bows of the ferry. He thought: this is no goddam good, I'm getting morbid. He was glad when the ferry berthed at Fishbourne and they drove off for Parkhurst. But his first sight of the tall, dreary blocks of the prison depressed him more than ever and he hoped fervently it wouldn't take him long to establish a line of communication with Chris Kilroe.

Noise, he found, alternated with silence and he couldn't make up his mind which was worse. The noise came in the workshops and at meal times, and along the echoing, clanging galleries. The silences were at night, when his cell mate was asleep while he lay sleepless in the narrow, hard bunk, staring up at the ceiling. He was by temperament unsuited for this kind of job. Everything grated on him, the proximity of his fellow-prisoners, the total lack of privacy, the mannerisms of his cell mate, the belch you came to expect every night before he went to sleep, a kind of long-drawn, vulgar good night trumpet-call. The crudely salacious jokes, the smell of sweat, the small cruelties of the gaolers, overworked and harrassed men who lived under more or less constant threat of physical violence from a percentage of the cons. The feeling of being cut off from your own kind.

There had, of course, been no contact with the Governor. Packard wondered how much, if anything, the ordinary prison officers knew about him. Whether they knew anything or not, they were totally impersonal and his treatment was precisely the same as any of the other cons, possibly a little tougher because of his supposed crime. No one liked his sort in a prison.

Meanwhile not much progress had been made, except that he had identified Chris Kilroe fairly quickly. As one of the big-time inmates, a man who had made a record target, he had been pointed out to Packard during an exercise period. Kilroe was a long, thin gangling sort of man with glasses, a weak chin and mouth and a nervous manner, taking his exercise separately—since the attempt to spring him—under extra heavy guard. This of course was not by way of punishment. As Packard's informant said, 'Kilroe didn't do anything he could be punished for, like. The reverse.'

'So he's being treated like anyone else?'

The man nodded. 'Except security-wise outside his cell—in case there's another try, see.'

Indeed, the man went on, the whole prison was on edge, geared up for that other try. Kilroe himself looked dead scared, as though he was in constant fear, not perhaps of another attempt at springing him, but, as Forbes had suggested, of some attempt from inside the prison to teach him a lesson in co-operation.

Packard could find no way of getting into contact with Kilroe but it seemed that the Governor was well aware of this aspect of the problem and two days later, when the other man in Packard's cell came up for release, his place was taken by Chris Kilroe.

From then on the campaign lines were easy enough.

'It's a small world right enough,' Kilroe said, rubbing at the non-existent chin. 'Who'd have thought it, eh?'

'Come again?'

'The bird. Lois Chailey.'

Packard's acting was good. 'Mean to say you know her?'

'No, but...well, know who's bird she is, do you?'

Packard shook his head. 'No. Should I?'

'She didn't tell you?'

Packard looked away. 'The charge was rape,' he said in a sulky tone. 'She didn't have the chance to tell me who her friends were.'

'No, well, I can see that.' Kilroe's eyes met his briefly then turned downwards. 'She's Brett Burgoyne's girl.'

'Who's he, then?'

Kilroe looked surprised. 'Mean to say you don't know?'

'I don't mix with the kind of people you probably do. I've never been in this sort of situation before, Kilroe. And I don't want to be again.'

'You read the papers, though.'

'So what?'

Kilroe made a sound of impatience. Packard watched the tic that kept his right eyelid on the move. 'The Hatton Garden job. What I done too. Burgoyne's on the run for that.'

'Oh?' Packard didn't show any interest; his line was that he was utterly wrapped up in his own misery, his own captivity.

'I don't remember all the names I read about.'

'Maybe not, but you better remember this one,' Kilroe said significantly. 'Brett's dangerous. You screw his girl, you get what's coming to you. Doesn't matter how long you're inside for, you got to come out one day, haven't you?'

Dully Packard said, 'I see what you mean. Where is this Burgoyne?'

'Like I told you, he's on the run. He...escaped a few months ago. Not from here—from Wandsworth it was. Don't ask me where he is now. Out of the country, like as not. In fact I reckon he must be.'

'Why's that?'

Kilroe shrugged. 'That's the aim always, when a con gets away with it. Stands to reason. It's safer, isn't it?'

'I suppose so. If he can *get* out.'

'There's ways and means,' Kilroe said indifferently. He didn't say any more about Burgoyne after that but the line of communication had been established and for the time being Packard left it where it was. Over the next few evenings he got to know Chris Kilroe pretty well. Kilroe was a shallow man with his fears very much on the surface but he was also an obstinate one and Packard soon saw that he wasn't going to give anything away and that in the interest of speed the lines of the campaign must shift a little so that those basic fears of Kilroe's, and the fact that he was conditioned already to expect some kind of assault, could be made to play their full part.

Some nights later Packard let Kilroe go to sleep then in the early hours he got softly out of his bunk, which was the lower one, and leaned his forearms on Kilroe's bunk and hissed into the man's ear, 'Chris, wake up. I want a word with you.'

Kilroe jerked into life. 'What the bloody—'

'Okay, take it easy. It's only me, Chris. Henry Paul Perkins. Right?'

'I don't get it. What you on about?' There was puzzlement in Kilroe's voice, and again the fear. 'I know your name, don't I?'

'Yes, you know it all right. But like I didn't know Brett Burgoyne, you don't know *me*. Do you?'

'No...not before I was put in your cell. I—'

'That's as it should be, Chris.'

'Look...I don't get all this, I—'

'It's right you shouldn't know me. You weren't meant to, Chris. But I knew all about Brett Burgoyne. And I'll tell you something else, Chris. I know Adam Fast and Rollo and I know all about the Sibley Boys. I know about the escape racket, Chris. You can't tell me anything I don't know. Except where Brett Burgoyne is. And I know you can tell me that. If you want to, that is.'

Kilroe's voice was a hoarse croak. 'How...how d'you know all this?'

Packard said, 'Listen, Chris. It's true I haven't been inside before. But on the other hand, that's only been because I've never been caught. I'm not talking about rape. My game's protection. Not in London. In Glasgow. And not in the name of Paul Henry Perkins. Now, after I was copped on the rape charge, Chris, I naturally got my lawyer lined up, didn't I, and once when he came to see me he told me a man called Adam Fast had been in touch with him because he knew my reputation and thought I could be useful

102

to him. Fast made a very nice little offer. Which was: in return for services rendered, he would spring me—after I'd done what he wanted—and get me out of the country together with a very nice reward payable in the currency of the country he got me to. With me so far?'

Kilroe nodded; he seemed to be past speaking.

'Well, now you'll want to know what it was I had to do, won't you?'

Again Kilroe nodded and in the dim lighting Packard saw the gleam of fear in his eyes. Packard said, 'First I'd better explain a little more. Mr Fast knew it was a safe enough bet that I'd land up in one or other of the gaols where the Hatton Garden boys were doing their time. After all, they're pretty widely spread. It's just chance that I've turned up in your parish, Chris. Not a happy chance for you, though. You see, my job for Mr Fast is to find out where Brett Burgoyne is, and also where he's hidden a large slice of the loot from that Hatton Garden robbery. Mr Fast is really most anxious to know, Chris. And he knows for absolutely certain that *you* know. It wouldn't have been half so helpful if I'd been sent to any other prison.'

Kilroe licked his lips. 'Suppose I *don't* know?' he asked.

'Oh, but you do. You know where he intended to make for, if he got away. If you don't tell me, Chris, so I can send it back through the grapevine as soon as I'm allowed visitors, I'm afraid I shall have to do you over very, very thoroughly indeed.'

Kilroe began whining. 'You won't get the chance. I'll report all this to the Governor.'

'No, you won't, Chris, because all this is going to take place here and now. Right at this moment, I'm between you and the Governor.'

'You lay a hand on me, mate, and you'll be inside the rest of your life.'

Packard grinned. 'No, I won't and you know it. Mr Fast keeps to his bargains. Wherever they send me, however long they sentence me to, I'll be out by Christmas. And safe. You—you'll be a cripple—and that *will* be for the rest of your life. Got it, Chris? I haven't any orthodox weapons, but I don't need them. I learned quite a lot in Glasgow. Well, what d'you say, Chris?'

NINE

Chris Kilroe was soft centred and he broke pretty fast after Packard had put on a little more pressure. Brett Burgoyne, he said, had arranged for a big cut of the diamonds to be smuggled out of the country to a fence of his own choosing in the Netherlands. This had been carried out by a trusted friend of Burgoyne's, a seaman aboard a Dutch coaster sailing regularly from the Tyne to the Hook of Holland and back. The fence, whose name Kilroe didn't know—and Packard believed he was genuinely ignorant on this point—would arrange for the conversion of the cash proceeds into *lira* which would in due course be paid over to Burgoyne in Naples.

'And that's where Burgoyne'll be now?' Packard asked.

'So far as I know, yes. That's where he meant to go, anyway.'

'Address?'

Kilroe shook his head. 'I don't know

that. Just that it was somewhere in Naples, or could be near Naples. I don't think he knew himself just where he'd fetch up.'

'Or he could even have told you that just to throw you off the beam. He could be in Timbuctoo.'

'I don't think so. I think he was giving me the real truth when he told me what he was going to do.'

'Why?'

'Because we'd always been friends, the three of us. He wouldn't ever do me out of my share.'

'So it's a case of honour among thieves...in a very literal sense?'

Kilroe shrugged. 'Call it that if you want. Like I said, we was friends. Real *mates*. He wouldn't ever have done anything like that, not to me or Morrissey.'

'All right,' Packard said. Kilroe was currently dropping Bret Burgoyne right smack in the dirt and he knew it, but there was no point in forcing the fact on his attention. 'So he meant to go to Naples and that's where he's most likely to be now.' He paused, eyeing Kilroe speculatively. 'Has he got contacts there?'

'Yes,' Kilroe said. 'Plenty. The right sort, too.'

'Meaning?'

'Well, see, he'd been out there as a young kid—in the British Army, just after the Italians packed it in. He got to know people in the rackets. Made himself a pile of cash as a kid private and come out richer than a Field Marshal. He went back for a long spell after the war and met up with his old mates again and he's kept up ever since. He goes a lot on Italy—almost made himself into an Eyetie. He can pass as one easy, any time he wants. Got all the mannerisms, as well as the lingo.'

'I see.' Packard recalled those photographs, recalled that decidedly Italian look. 'He never told you who those mates were, I suppose?'

Kilroe shook his head. 'No, he didn't do that.' He was silent for a moment, biting anxiously at his lower lip. Then he asked, 'Fast going to do him, is he? Brett won't know it was me put that bastard on to him, will he?'

Packard smiled. 'You can set your mind at rest,' he said. 'If I get to Brett Burgoyne in time, no one's going to do him.'

Kilroe's mouth dropped open. 'If *you* get to him in time, did you say?'

'I did. I'll be seeing the Governor in the

morning, early, and by the time you've had your breakfast I'll be on my way to London. And then Naples. I'm sorry, but what I told you isn't true. I'm no con and I have no hook-up with Adam Fast. I'm strictly on the other side and my job is to get to Burgoyne before Fast does. What you've done is to help me save your mate's life, in effect. And ultimately your own as well.'

'I don't get all this,' Kilroe muttered. He looked rocked, and scared all over again.

Packard repeated the salient points and added, 'Now one other thing. You're never going to open your mouth about this conversation or about me at all—except to the authorities if ever you have to. What I'm getting at is this: nothing is to go outside the gates by the grapevine. And in case you haven't already guessed why, I'll just tell you. If you open your yap, Chris Kilroe, Adam Fast is going to get you sooner or later—even inside a British gaol. You know very well that's true. You've been sentenced already for what you did. That can't be added to. One day, you'll come out—it won't be all that long if you behave. When that day comes, you won't want Adam Fast and the Sibley

Boys breathing down your neck, will you? It's in your own best interests to clam right up and let me see to it that all the mob get the chop.'

In the morning at first call Packard asked to see the Governor on an urgent matter and the officer he spoke to understood perfectly. In the Governor's office Packard made his report and asked for immediate transport to London. He added, 'I'd better go out the way I came in—as a con on transfer. I don't want my face to be seen at large around this way.'

Within fifteen minutes he was escorted by two prison officers to a police car and they started off at once for Fishbourne and the car ferry to Portsmouth. Things looked different this way round, though even his escort didn't know just who or what he was. Two hours after leaving Portsmouth they were entering London and making once again for Pentonville. In Pentonville, Packard was taken direct to the Governor's office where he made a telephone call, a brief one, to Forbes and changed back into his own clothing. Then, to complete the security picture, he was taken in a prison van back to the Old Bailey, his face hidden again by his jacket; this time, instead of a cell, he was taken to a private office where he spent a half-hour with a cigarette, a cup of coffee and a charming woman P.C before emerging into the street as James Packard. He took a taxi to Throgmorton Street where he had a longish session with Forbes.

'It's going to be dead tricky,' Forbes said after Packard had passed the whole story. He drummed his fingers on the desk. 'Like looking for that needle in a hundred haystacks. D'you know Naples at all, James?'

'I've been there, but I wouldn't say I know it. I do know what you mean, though. It's a real rabbit-warren.'

'That's an understatement. There's another point, too. You're going to stand out a bit.'

'I don't see that,' Packard objected. 'I won't be the only Englishman in Naples, and Burgoyne doesn't know me so far as I'm aware.'

'That's just it, James—*so far as you're aware*. You're known to Adam Fast and this man Rollo, and I'm always terribly conscious of grapevines. I dare say we could fix you up a little,' he added, looking critically at Packard's face. That long chin was always a trifle difficult to hide.

Packard shook his head. 'I don't like disguises, you know that, Colonel. They can't always be kept up, and a man needs to wash now and again.'

'But look, James—you say Burgoyne has these Italian contacts. Now, it's only too likely Fast knows that as well as Kilroe. Fast could be casting an eye in that direction by now. If so, you could be spotted a mile off—even though they believe you're dead.'

'True, but I don't believe Fast *does* know about the Italian link-up. If he did, why hasn't he had Naples tooth-combed before now?'

'Maybe he has,' Forbes said, 'without striking any oil.'

'Which makes it even more difficult for us, of course.' Packard frowned. 'Well, anyway, we have to do something and do it quickly. And the only thing we can do, in my view, is to attack more or less openly. That is, I'll have to get to Naples and do my best to latch myself on to Burgoyne even if it means using that grapevine you're so worried about. But in this case, the domestic Naples grapevine.'

'You mean, let it be known you want to talk to Burgoyne?'

'Yes, just that—and also why.'

'But damn it, man—he'll know the score for himself! He's not that green. He won't want to be arrested, either.'

'I didn't mean that. I meant a phony 'why.' I'm just trying to dream something up.'

Forbes said, 'If that's what you're after, the answer's obvious: the girl—Lois Chailey. She needs him. He's going to be a daddy. How's that?'

'Lousy. Oh, it *could* work, I suppose, but...' He slammed a fist into his palm. 'I *could* use her as bait. Take her over with me in the flesh. Let her be seen around, keep an eye on her and let her lead me to the boy-friend. I think we can assume that by now Fast has leaked the word through that she's dead, just in case the information flushes Burgoyne out. So when Burgoyne gets to hear she's in Naples, whether he still loves her or not he's going to be Godalmighty curious, isn't he?'

'Yes, I'd say so,' Forbes said. He wrinkled the flesh around his eyes, considering some point. 'I still think you should arrive in Naples incognito. In fact I insist on that. You'll be able to watch more effectively.' He pressed a switch in the intercom on his desk and spoke to Felicity Teal. 'Tell Marlon to come over right away,' he said, and let the switch go. Pierre Marlon was CWA's make-up expert. 'There's one other little piece of cover you can take along with you,' Forbes went on to Packard. 'I think you'll enjoy it.'

'What is it?' Packard asked suspiciously.

'Miss Teal. She happens to know Naples pretty well, also the country around. I'm sure she'd like a holiday...with you, James.' He smiled brightly. 'I rather like being a fairy godmother. I'll have accommodation booked for you in the Hotel Anzio, it's a romantic kind of setting, up on the heights opposite Vesuvius...'

Forbes produced his photographic studies of Brett Burgoyne once again and then made a phone call while they waited for Pierre Marlon. He arranged for Lois Chailey to be brought back next day from Ipswich. She would leave for Naples the day after her arrival in London and Packard, going out ahead with Felicity via Rome, would discreetly shadow her

113

arrival and thereafter keep a watch on her. All this, of course, depended on the girl's own willingness to co-operate, but Packard didn't doubt that willingness. That night, with his face considerably and very artistically re-arranged so that he had a slightly flattened nose, heavier eyebrows, and a vicious-looking pencil-line moustache, he picked Felicity up from her flat and took her to the BEA terminal. On the way out in the airport bus Felicity said, 'James, I haven't mentioned this before, but are we supposed to be having an affair?'

He grinned. 'Didn't Forbes instruct you fully?'

'You know what Forbes is like,' she said.

'Oh—very military still. Yes. So he left it to me, did he?'

She nodded. She was very close to him, closer than she needed to be, and he liked her scent. He said, 'The idea is we're *supposed* to be, yes. And you can interpret that any way you like. I know how I'm going to interpret it,' he added.

She gave a quiet little chuckle. 'I'm so glad,' she said.

TEN

They touched down at Rome's Leonardo da Vinci airport at 0635 and in the interest of doing all possible to fox any speculation by third parties they rejected the Alitalia flight for Naples in favour of the railways. They reached Naples in time for a drink and lunch at a super-luxury restaurant. They took their time over lunch and then spent the afternoon sightseeing, like any couple on holiday, just walking around the town and getting the feel of it and keeping their eyes open. Packard always liked to get his geography established as early as possible in the game. It could mean the difference between life and death when the crunch came. Meanwhile, sightseeing with Felicity was an enjoyable interlude. The day was fresh and fine, not too hot, and their spirits were high. The surroundings seemed to suit Felicity, to fit her personality. She blossomed. They covered as much ground as they could, down by the docks, in the glittering shopping area, contrasting the wealth of the fine streets with the breadline poverty and dirt in the side streets that lay so close, in geographic terms, to the spenders' paradise. They stopped for coffee in a pavement café, later for drinks in another. They came to the San Carlo Opera House.

'Madame Butterfly,' Felicity remarked. 'Have you seen it?'

Packard said, 'I'm not much of a one for opera.'

'This is the chance of a lifetime,' she said and there was a touch of wistfulness. 'James, this is the San Carlo! You simply can't pass it up.'

'Haven't you ever been before?'

'Yes,' she said, 'I have, but I was thinking of you.'

He grinned. 'Mean to improve my education, is that it?'

'Well, you can't deny you could do with it. You're a bit of a Philistine when it comes to the arts, let's face it.'

He said, 'That's the way I mean to stay. I'll buy you an expensive dinner instead, my darling.'

Next morning after a late breakfast in

116

bed—and after Packard, following Pierre Marlon's instructions in the matter, had attended to his face—they wandered again around the city and at 1355, Packard, alone this time, was sitting behind a newspaper in the SITA air terminal in the Via Victor Emanuele. He watched as the passengers from the BEA flight to Capodichino airport came through. Lois Chailey was among them. He saw her looking around, furtively, doing what Forbes would have told her not to do—trying to spot him. She looked straight at him but thank God there was no recognition in her face...so maybe she had got the right idea after all—or maybe his slight disguise was more effective than he had dared to hope. She turned away from him and spoke to an airline official, who seemed to be giving her some directions, for she nodded several times, and smiled, and then walked with a small handcase out of the building.

Packard folded up his newspaper and got to his feet. He followed casually, lighting a cigarette. Lois Chailey walked quickly, glancing around, getting her bearings. Packard knew she had been booked into the Caserta Hotel, which was little more than a step away. No one was taking any apparent interest in the girl and certainly no one other than himself was following her. He watched her go into the hotel foyer and he paused, looking around as if uncertain himself of his directions, and watched her talking to a young man at the reception desk and then taking possession of a key.

So far so good.

He moved on. She would know what to do. He went back to his own hotel by taxi. Felicity was sitting on a terrace, looking out across the city spread below them, with Vesuvius away beyond, smoking just a little, and Capri with its brilliant blue surround. She asked, 'Well?'

'She's checked in,' he told her. 'She didn't seem to recognise me.'

'Think she will, tonight?'

He said, 'If we follow directions implicitly, yes.'

She nodded dreamily. 'It's lovely, up here,' she said. 'I don't want this to end, ever. I simply daren't even *think* about Throgmorton Street...and that bloody District Line in the rush hour.'

At 1900 hours Packard and Felicity were sitting in La Cigale, a French-run café in the Via Partenope. They were inside, not on the pavement, and they were in a discreet corner where they couldn't be overheard. At 1915 hours precisely Lois Chailey came in and sat at a table nearby; she had given a quick look around as she came in but once again there had been no hint of recognition. Packard and Felicity carried on talking quietly, then suddenly Packard reached into a pocket and brought out his cigarette case. He began slapping his pockets and after a moment said loudly, 'Damn and blast, I've left my flipping lighter behind, would you believe it? Got a match, darling?'

He saw the girl stiffen. Felicity said, 'Sorry, no matches.'

Packard met Lois Chailey's eye and grinned. She got up and moved across towards their table. She said, 'I'm ever so sorry, I couldn't help hearing. Here.' She handed Packard a lighter.

'Oh,' he said, 'thanks very much, love.'

She said, 'That's all right. D'you know, I haven't been here long, but it's so nice to hear an English voice. I can't speak any Italian and there don't seem to be many English people here, do there?'

'There don't, love,' Packard said. 'It's

all this economy, that's what it is. People come strictly on business. Care to join us, would you?'

'I'd love to,' Lois said. 'Thank you very much.' She sat, a little diffidently, unsure of herself in a strange land, suddenly appearing much more provincial than she had back in Britain. She said, 'Oh, by the way, my name's Chailey, Lois Chailey.' She came out with that loud and clear, as per instructions. Already the scene was being set.

'How do,' Packard said. 'Harry Stevens... and Miss Carr.' He winked. 'We're engaged, love.'

'Oh, how nice,' she said, and blushed. Packard had a feeling all this was going to be too much for her, that she would be in danger of giving things away. Suddenly, jerkily, she recalled the rest of her instructions and asked, 'Where are you from, Mr Stevens?'

'Brum.'

'Oh. I'm from London really, though I've been down in Bognor for quite a while.' A waiter came up and Packard asked what she would like and she asked for a straight Martini Bianca. When the drink came they chatted about Bognor and

120

Birmingham and London then Packard said, 'Well, seeing we've met up, love, you're more than welcome to come along and look around with us if you want.'

She said, 'Yes, I'd like that.'

He stood up. 'Come on, then.'

They went out into the Via Partenope. 'You know what you have to do,' Packard told her, dropping the act he had put on inside. 'Just let yourself be seen, that's all. It's quite simple. Don't be shy of giving your name whenever the chance crops up, and if you get a chance of dropping the name of Burgoyne around town—take it. I'll leave that to you. And remember this: all the way from now on, we'll be around. The moment you make contact with Burgoyne, we'll know. And believe me,' he added kindly, 'it's the best way for him. The only safe way.'

She nodded, but there were tears in her eyes now. She said. 'Colonel Forbes told me.'

'And you believe him...don't you, Lois?'

She said sadly, 'Yes...yes, I do.'

'That's fine. Keep on believing it, Lois. Once we get our hands on all the Sibley Boys and Adam Fast in particular, Burgoyne's going to come through all this one day. Just do your part and you won't need to worry.'

When later the girl walked on alone Felicity said, 'James, she's terribly nice. Makes me feel quite motherly.'

He said, 'Don't start thinking of yourself as a mother just yet, Felicity...but I do know what you mean. She looks sort of lost out here.'

'Yes.' She gave him a critical look. 'I hope *your* feelings are fatherly ones, James, and nothing more.'

He laughed. 'I'll let you know the answer to that one later on. I have to go now or I'll lose her.'

'Where are you going to spend the night?'

'Asked with a feeling heart! Not in bed with her, anyway. Forbes wouldn't wear that.'

She clicked her tongue. 'Oh, you're impossible. But seriously...the night seems to me the time of danger for that girl.'

'It's a chance we have to take,' he said. 'It was too risky to book her into our hotel—you know that. And since she's going to move around plenty, anyone who wants to get at her is going to see a much safer chance that way than by breaking into a hotel bedroom. Anyway—I hope so.' He bent and kissed her. 'See you, Felicity.'

'See you,' she said, and then watched his tall figure as he moved away behind Lois Chailey, who was sauntering along some way ahead. She felt a small shiver of apprehension as she watched, felt also a nagging little twinge of jealousy that she knew inside herself was unnecessary and also presumptive. She had no claim on James Packard in fact, however much she would have liked to have.

She turned away after that and found a taxi to take her back to the heights above the town, out from the close air and the smells of congested Naples, and she dined alone and then once again sat out on the terrace in the soft night air and wondered how and where Packard would pass a very long night on guard.

Lois Chailey had struggled for the inside of a minute with the lock of the left-hand door of the large wardrobe in her bedroom. It was a monumental affair, divided into two complete sections and she had only tried to open it out of the sheerest curiosity—for her small handcase didn't hold anything like enough to fill the one side that was unlocked. So she shrugged and left it; the hotel probably kept spare blankets in the locked side, she thought...

She went to bed early, wondering about Brett Burgoyne, wondering, as she had kept on wondering, whether or not she was really doing the best thing. Brett certainly wasn't going to see it that way; it would be the big betrayal in his eyes and he couldn't be blamed for that. *He* wouldn't be worried about Adam Fast and the Sibley Boys. He'd say he could deal with them himself, if ever they turned up. He wasn't going to thank her for putting him back inside.

But, to her, that was better than his being killed by the Sibley Boys.

Maybe he *could* be made to see it that way...

It was a long time before she dropped off to sleep but when she did find sleep it was a heavy one, almost a drugged one. She went out like a light. Her bed was alongside the big wardrobe and the man hidden in it heard the heavy breathing. He gave it another half-hour to be on the safe side and then very gently and quietly he turned the key, eased the door open, stopping when there was a creaking noise, then going on fractionally until he was able to come right out into the open. Carefully he shut the door again and locked it and put the key in his pocket. He bent over the bed, scarcely breathing himself, a dark bulky shadow listening out for any change in the pattern of the girl's breathing. Then he backed away, and turned, and groped around the room until he found Lois Chailey's handbag. He hadn't quite got to it when he had an accident. He cannoned into a chair and nearly went down on his face. Nearly but not quite. The noise woke the girl but the man moved like a flash and he was at her throat before she could make a sound. He squeezed hard and went on squeezing. He was a strong man and a violent one and inclined sometimes to panic, which made him overdo things.

ELEVEN

In cover in the small courtyard behind the Caserta Hotel, Packard caught a muted scraping sound from above and a moment later he heard the quick descending footsteps on the fire escape and he picked out the dark, moving shape of a man. There was no light in the courtyard and he moved out from behind what smelt like a pigswill area and made quietly and unseen towards the bottom of the fire escape.

He had his gun in his hand but he never had a chance to use it. As he reached the metal steps the man became aware of him and reacted instantly and lashed out with a foot. He caught Packard on the point of the jaw and as Packard went over backwards he was away down the side alley leading into a roadway off the Via Partenope. By the time Packard was on his feet again it was too late. He ran down the alley and up into the Via Partenope, then turned and went along the side road in the other direction. There was no sign of anyone. The night was quiet and still and deserted.

Cursing, he went back into the courtyard and climbed up the fire escape. He knew he could be worrying over nothing, that the man could have been no more than a petty thief with no interest in Lois Chailey, but he didn't really believe this because the coincidence would have been a trifle much.

He stopped at the fourth floor, the floor on which Lois Chailey's room was; she had already told him the fire escape ran close to her window, that the window at the end of the corridor next to her room gave access to it. Packard went through the window quietly and padded along the corridor. Turning to his right, he found the girl's room. He tried the door but it was locked. Bolted too, by the feel of it. He tapped gently; there was no reply.

He didn't particularly want to bring the management into this.

He went back along the passage to the fire escape and looked to his left. The girl's window was wide open. If he was right about the bolts, then the man, if he had been in Lois Chailey's room, must have come out this way. Packard swung himself onto the handrail of the fire escape's landing, balanced himself against the wall of the building, and reached out slowly and carefully towards the sill of the bedroom window. He got a grip on the wall's edge and stretched out his foot towards the sill. Within a minute he was standing on the sill. He bent and jumped lightly down inside the room. He saw the shape of the girl beneath a sheet, saw the long fair hair spread out on the pillow, and he called to her as he moved across.

There was no answer.

Forty minutes later he was in Felicity Teal's room in the Hotel Anzio. The time was still only 0130 hours. He told her all he knew, which wasn't much. He said, 'She was strangled. The man got clear away. There seemed to be nothing touched in the room, except that her handbag was open. Not knowing what she had in it, I can't say what, if anything, was taken.'

'Money?'

'There was money there—nothing much, three thousand *lira*, under a couple of pounds, and some loose change. If you're thinking that was the motive, you can forget it. A small-time thief wouldn't have left even that much.'

Her face was white and drawn. 'What was the motive, then, James?'

He snapped, 'You tell me. My guess is, it was Adam Fast making sure anyone interested knew his threats were always carried out. She could have been recognised before she left UK. Anyway, that'll have to wait. We have things to do right now, Felicity, and you'd better get some clothes on because I want your help. It won't be nice but it's necessary.'

'What is?'

He said, 'We have to get her away from that hotel, that's what.'

She stared at him, her face going whiter than ever. 'What do you mean, James?'

He said in a hard, tight voice, 'Look, Felicity. If we leave her there to be found in the morning by the chambermaid, I doubt if I have to tell you the police are in right away—'

'James, don't be—'

'All right, all right, I was just underlining the point. Or trying to. The point being that once the police are on this job, nothing on this earth is going to stop the press getting hold of the story. And when that happens, whoever did that killing is going to know the score, right?'

She was puzzled. 'I don't follow. Or I don't think I do.'

'Think again, then,' he snapped. He was badly on edge, she could see. 'Lois Chailey's death very probably closes the deal for the killer and whoever was behind him, which for my money is the Sibley Boys. The thing's done and that's that. They don't know *I'm* here—they may make the assumption in the circumstances, of course, but they still don't *know*. She could have got out of that underground stream and I could have drowned, right? In any case, they're going to withdraw—after they've found Burgoyne, anyway. And that may not be so long, once the news breaks. That news could flush Brett Burgoyne to the surface, right where the Sibley Boys want him. And they could get to him before we do. So I want to fox things up a little more. I want more time, amongst other things. Get it now?'

'I get the drift,' she said. She was already dressing. 'But what do you mean to *do?*'

'I mean to get Lois out of that room,' he told her, 'and hide her.'

'Hide her?' She stared at him as she pulled on a pair of slacks. 'For God's sake, James...where?'

'I don't know yet. It'll come to me. But if we can do it, can you imagine what it's going to do to the Sibley Boys when they get to hear there was no case—because there was no body?'

'Yes,' she said. 'Yes, I can see that, all right. How do we do it, though?'

'For a start, there's a Fiat estate car parked down below, outside the garages.

It won't take me long to get inside that and start it. If we hurry, we can be back before anyone's up and about. No more questions for now, Felicity. We'll do the rest of the thinking on the move.'

TWELVE

It took Packard just three minutes to fiddle the Fiat's lock and another two to get the car started after he and Felicity had manhandled it quietly clear of the hotel and down the road that sloped towards the town. After this they drove fast for the Via Partenope and left the Fiat parked in the side street at the end of the alley that led to the courtyard.

Then they climbed the fire escape.

At the fourth landing Packard once again bridged the gap into Lois's room and jumped through. He went quickly to the door and unlocked it and slid the bolts back. Felicity was waiting. She came in and he closed the door quietly behind her, locking it once again.

He flicked his torch on, shone the beam

131

on the body in the bed. He heard Felicity's gasp, saw the drained look in her face, the shock and horror in her eyes. She said, 'Oh, James, it's...horrible.'

'Yes,' he said, 'it is. But they're not going to get away with it, Felicity. Can you cope for now?'

Slowly, she nodded, though she hung back from the bed. 'I'll manage,' she said.

'Good girl.' He pulled the sheet away once more. In death the body looked small and fragile. They both tried not to look at the distorted face, at the rounded bruises on the throat. Packard said briefly, his voice sharp with his own revulsion for their task, 'You take the legs. Wait a moment, though.' He went across and unlocked the door again and opened it. Then he went back to the bed and lifted the girl's shoulders. Felicity lifted as well and they carried the body towards the door, setting it down for a moment while Packard pulled the door to behind him quietly. Then they picked Lois up again and went back along the passage to the window and the fire escape. Carefully they went down, pausing for Felicity to rest briefly at each of the landings. Unseen, unheard, they took their burden across the courtyard and down the alley to the Fiat and they had set it on the ground for Packard to open up the rear doors when the policeman sauntered out from a doorway to their left.

'One moment, *Signore,*' he said. 'What is it you are carrying?'

Packard's gun was already in his hand. 'I'll advise you not to call for assistance,' he said gently in Italian, 'nor to make any other fuss, but what we're carrying is, as you've already seen for yourself, a body. Do just as I tell you, friend, and you won't be reduced to the same condition.' He was aware of Felicity's consternation, of her astonishment at what he had said. He went on, 'Now—give the lady a hand with the body. And move!'

He snapped the order out and gestured threateningly with his gun. The policeman watched him narrowly but did as he was told. When the body was stowed Packard ordered the man to get in the front and told Felicity to drive. He slid in the back seat himself and kept his gun in the policeman's neck.

The man asked, 'Where are you going?'

Packard grinned. 'Now I'm going to surprise you,' he said. 'Where else should we go but to—police headquarters?'

He felt the policeman's astonishment. The man half turned in his seat, his eyes puzzled. 'You are serious?'

'But definitely. Frankly, you haven't left me any choice, by turning up just at the wrong moment. I'm strictly on the level,' he added, 'but for certain reasons which I'll be only too pleased—now I'm forced to, that is—to explain to your *commandante*, I had to avoid any unpleasantness at the scene of the crime. Off you go, Felicity.'

She started up and followed the policeman's directions. The man's whole attitude suggested to Packard that he thought the Englishman was mad; he kept looking at him over his shoulder, as though he feared the madman might discharge the gun—and was obviously much relieved to find himself still unharmed when the Fiat turned into a courtyard behind police headquarters. As the car stopped Packard put away his gun and said, 'Now you can call all the help you need, friend,' and climbed out.

'Where,' the police officer in charge asked helplessly, 'did you intend taking the body, *Signore?*'

Packard shrugged. 'Wherever I could find that was safe for as long as possible.' he said. 'You understand, I hadn't had the time to make the sort of reconnaissance that was really called for. I was simply hoping to find somewhere in the countryside around—you know?'

The officer shrugged eloquently. 'It is possible you might have found such a place.' He drummed his fingers on his desk, a gesture that reminded Packard of Forbes back in London. 'This is a curious story you have told me, *Signore*. Is there anything you have to add, before I ring Signor Pampanelli?'

'Nothing. You have the lot.'

'It is very extraordinary.'

'Maybe it is. But you've heard of the Criminal Warfare Agencies, haven't you?'

'But yes, certainly. This I have told you—also that I have worked with Signor Pampanelli.' Pampanelli was CWA's Rome boss. 'It is still...very extraordinary.'

Wearily Packard said, 'Look, Signor Malfa, I've told you, haven't I, I wanted no publicity. This was the only way I could make sure of that—I mean, removing the body. I didn't expect to walk slap into one of your men while I was doing it.'

'If in the first place you had called the police—'

'And had a swarm of you buzzing around the Caserta Hotel? That would have been a big help! I'm sorry, Signor Malfa, but my experience of the police in many countries all over the world tends to make me doubt if they could ever react anonymously in a situation like *that* would have become. So, you see, I had no alternative.' Packard looked pointedly at his watch. 'If you wouldn't mind ringing Pampanelli's home number? There's a little matter of a stolen Fiat—if I may remind you, *Signore*. I'd rather not be charged with that if it can be avoided, and the owner's liable to wake at any time now.'

The policeman threw up his hands in a gesture almost of despair, then took up his telephone and asked for the Rome number. Within ten minutes he was talking to Pampanelli—quickly, agitatedly, casting suspicious glances at Packard and Felicity meanwhile. There was much gesticulation, then a series of '*si's*' and nods of the head as he listened to Pampanelli. At last he put down the phone. 'Very well,' he said to Packard. 'I accept your identity.

136

Nevertheless, I must ask you both to hand me your passports pending a personal visit from Signor Pamapenelli.'

'Why?'

Malfa shrugged. 'A formality until you are positively and personally identified.'

'If you don't believe me, why say you accept my identity?'

He got an acid smile in return. 'I do not say I do not believe you. I wish for a little insurance, that is all. I have a wife and seven children...and a mother-in-law. I am not a rich man. I wish to protect my job and my pension. Your passports, please, *Signore.*'

CWA operators never left passports in hotel bedrooms. Packard and Felicity handed theirs over. Packard asked, 'Now can we go?'

The policeman nodded. 'Certainly. I will let you know when Signor Pampanelli arrives. In the meantime, any assistance you ask for will be given on request. I assure you of this. Please do not act in contravention of our laws. Before you go, there is the question of the body.'

'Yes. I'm going to ask you to keep it in the police morgue, *Signore,* and not on any account to allow the word to leak that

137

you have it here. I'm going to ask you to say nothing to anyone at all, other than Pampanelli, of what I have told you.'

Malfa sighed and said grudgingly, 'Very well, this I will see to. One moment.' He reached out again for his telephone, which had buzzed at him. After listening for a moment he cradled the handset in his shoulder and said to Packard, 'A Fiat has been reported stolen from the Hotel Anzio. This also I suppose I must see to.'

Packard smiled. 'If you wouldn't mind,' he said politely. 'I suggest you say it's been picked up...*not* in the vicinity of the Caserta Hotel, by the way...and you have it here. And we'll have to make our own way back. I'd rather not arrive at the hotel in a police car.'

Before speaking into the phone again the policeman said angrily, 'This is all very well, but you leave me with an unsolvable crime, *Signore!*'

'Don't worry too much,' Packard told him gently. 'Once we're out of the country, you can make a sudden diagnosis and write the crime off. I don't think car borrowing is extraditable.'

'I keep thinking,' Felicity said guiltily,

138

'of that poor girl. She came here to help us and that's what happens to her.'

'She knew the risks,' he pointed out. 'I know that doesn't help, of course. But at least we're in a position to get to grips with whoever did it. That's something.'

She said, 'Yes, it would be if it were true. But is it, James? We're right back where we started, if you ask me.'

'It may look that way at the moment,' he agreed as he helped himself to a second cup of coffee, 'but just wait till the murder fails to hit the news-stands. That's all. That aspect remains the same as ever, Felicity. In fact we're really in a stronger position, as things have turned out. I mean, as regards the police being in on this now. The way I'd hoped to play it, the body *could* have been found and that would have lost us fifty per cent of the mystery element. As things are now, the poor girl's vanished utterly.'

She said obstinately, 'I'm sick of this waiting game.'

'It hasn't been all that long yet.'

'It has for me. It doesn't seem right, considering what's happened. To Lois, I mean. To be sitting here doing nothing but play holidays while she's in that ghastly morgue like a criminal or a no-hoper or a suicide.'

'Felicity,' he said roughly, 'snap out of it, will you? We have a job to do. We're going to do it. We're doing it right now—even by waiting around. Don't you see?'

She said, 'No, I'm afraid I don't,' and he saw the way her hands were shaking, saw too the tears start to spill over from her eyes. She looked haunted and she was over-tired. She got up suddenly, knocking into the table and spilling some of his coffee. 'Watch it,' he said, half-humourously. She took no notice but turned away from him and went out of the room and across the foyer towards the lifts.

He shrugged and sat on, stirring his coffee thoughtfully. Felicity didn't come back; he hadn't really expected her to. After a while he got up and went up to her room and tapped on the door, but there was no answer. He went along to his own room to fetch a packet of cigarettes, then went down again in the lift. He went on waiting alone. He began to feel irritable at the way Felicity was behaving. Damn it all, he thought, she ought to know that an agent's life couldn't be all action. The waiting was a very necessary part. People had to be given time in which to fall into traps.

The only trouble was, he admitted ruefully to himself, there couldn't really be said to be an actual trap this time...

Just before 1300 hours, by which time Felicity had still not re-appeared, there was a phone call. Answering this, Packard was told that Signore Pampanelli had arrived at police headquarters and would Packard come along right away. He did so, by taxi. Pampanelli identified him and they had a brief conference. Pampanelli was of no particular help and Packard hadn't expected him to be; he had been contacted in advance by Forbes and had already said he had no knowledge of Brett Burgoyne or of anyone else concerned. He was more than a little put out at having to be dragged all the way from Rome by police formalities, as he called them, though he admitted that murder was murder and policemen, however high-ranking, were always susceptible to unemployment.

Packard went back to his hotel in a depressed state of mind, finding that after all his talk the waiting was beginning to get him down too. Still there was no sign of Felicity. He enquired casually at reception and was told by the clerk that he believed he had seen the English young lady going out, but he couldn't be entirely sure. Lunching alone after a couple of whiskies in the bar, Packard began to get a little worried. She was a capable enough girl, but then so had Lois Chailey been...could anything have happened, he wondered?

Thinking of Lois Chailey wasn't at all a good thing. He managed, morbidly, to convince himself that Felicity had come to some physical harm; and he was about to call police headquarters and ask for that assistance they'd promised, when she came into the dining-room smiling as though all the depression of the morning had evaporated.

Irrationally, he felt angry. Surlily he asked, 'Where the bloody hell have you been, for God's sake? And stop looking as if you've laid an egg.'

She sat down. 'Tired of waiting?' she asked demurely.

He glowered. 'If you really want to know, I've been worried about you.'

'About me? Oh, James, that's nice of you.'

'Is it?' He took a mouthful of scampi. 'Don't make a habit of getting me worried, just for the thrill it gives you! I'm serious, Felicity.' He reached out a hand to her. 'Don't go off on your own again.'

'All right,' she said. She was still smiling. 'But that would be a pity really, because if I don't, we're not going to get very far...just sitting around. Just waiting.'

He looked up sharply. 'Come on,' he said. 'What is it?'

She said, 'Only that I saw a man sitting outside a café drinking asti spumante.'

'Really.'

'Yes. I thought I recognised him.'

'Ex-boy-friend...or don't you always know them all right off?'

She flushed at that. 'That was quite unnecessary, James, and you know it. You're just being bloody-minded. I wish you wouldn't be, because this is serious. I thought I recognised him from your own detailed description, which I typed for Forbes. So acting like any tourist I took a snap without him realising. Here it is.'

She passed him a snap from her self-developing camera and he recognised Adam Fast.

THIRTEEN

'I waited in cover,' Felicity told him, 'looking in a shop window on the other side of the road a dozen yards down. I'm quite sure he didn't pay any attention to me.'

'How long did he stay there?'

'About ten minutes. Just under, actually.'

'Alone?'

'Yes, all the time. When he got up I followed him. But I'm afraid I lost him, James.'

'Uh-huh. Where?'

'Somewhere in the Via Roma. He could have gone into almost any of the shops. I waited for a while then thought it would be better if I came back here and told you about it. There was just no sign of him anywhere, you see.' She added. 'Sorry.'

He nodded. 'Well, it can't be helped, Felicity. Thanks for the snap.' He smiled at her. 'You haven't done so badly. At least we know he's here in Naples.'

'What do we do now?'

144

'Finish lunch,' he said. 'What else?'

'And after that?'

'Same as before. Carry on waiting. That's the way it goes.'

There were plenty of tourists around in the ruined city of Pompeii, below the great bulk of Vesuvius, still with its cap of smoke. They were chiefly French and German with a few Spanish, but Adam Fast didn't stand out among them as he got out of his self-drive hire car and started to poke about around the broken walls and the pavements and the lewd depictions of male Roman prowess. After a time he was joined, casually, by Rollo and the man called Bearsted and by two Italians and they all got into one of those conversations that arise when people with mutual interests meet in tourist spots. They continued walking around looking keen on the history that lay all about them. Adam Fast let drop the information that he had found himself a flat in a suburb of Naples and that he was looking forward to a long stay.

'Your country suits me nicely,' he murmured to one of the Italians.

The man smiled knowingly. 'More so

than Britain, perhaps?'

'At the moment, yes.' He paused. 'Well? What's the news from your end, Cino?'

Cino lifted his shoulders and spread his hands wide. 'All well. It is done. Unfortunately perhaps, in the process...' He gave a quick flick of his hand towards his throat and at the same time jerked his head.

Adam Fast stopped moving and turned to face Cino. His face darkening, he said, 'You mean...?'

Cino nodded. 'Yes, *Signore.*' Suddenly he looked doubtful. 'There was no instruction to the contrary, and it so happened the girl woke—'

'Why? Why did she wake?'

Cino shrugged. 'It happens,' he said placatingly. 'Girls wake in the night when—'

'When they hear a noise a clumsy fool has made.' Fast's tone was icy. 'That was it—wasn't it, Cino?'

The Italian bowed his head. 'This is possible, yes, but it was such a very little noise.'

'Enough, though! I thought you said all was well? Did you find...what you were looking for?'

Cino did his best to make a virtue of necessity. 'No,' he said, 'because there was nothing to find. There was no information about this man Burgoyne at all, thus we can assume, can we not, that the girl had no knowledge of him and had come simply on the chance that she might meet him? Is this not so?'

Adam Fast was now pale with anger, with the effort of holding it down. He tapped Cino. He said, 'I can't blame you for not finding what wasn't there, but God help you if you overlooked what *was* there. Meanwhile, another death doesn't help—especially her death! You know very well—'

'But *Signore*... I knew the intention was to kill her eventually—'

'Eventually, yes.' Fast stared up at a scene of ancient debauchery and felt a pang of envy for the Roman way of life. 'Eventually—that was the whole point! She can't lead us to Burgoyne now—can she, Cino?'

The Italian muttered, 'I am sorry, *Signore*. What I did was of necessity.'

'Owing to your own bloody incompetence in the first place,' Fast said witheringly, his fat body trembling.

Cino took the insult and then, brightening, said, 'But *Signore,* when the news breaks, it may bring Burgoyne out into the open. She was, after all, his *inamorata.'*

Fast considered the point then said grudgingly, 'It could work that way. On the other hand, if he suspects who's behind it, it could drive him down deeper—couldn't it?'

'I would say, not necessarily, *Signore.* Burgoyne may wish to avenge...in which case it will be he who seeks out you, rather than you him.'

'Stop trying to justify yourself,' Adam Fast snapped irritably. 'And in future stick to your orders. If you don't, I'll give you just one guess what happens to you.' He stared into the Italian's face again, his own flabby cheeks wobbling. 'I suppose you left no clues behind, did you—and no one saw you coming or going?'

Blandly Cino lied. 'No one, *Signore.* You need have no worries.'

Adam Fast turned away as a group of Germans wandered in their direction. Not looking at the others he said in a soft voice, 'This is going to need more consideration after this evening's papers are out. We meet in my flat at...let's say seven-thirty. All of you.' He walked on, hot and tired and dust-covered and with a raging thirst beginning to develop. And a nagging worry. Sure, Lois Chailey had had to die, should have died in that Scottish stream—and he still had to find out how she had managed to achieve that seeming miracle—but it would have been far, far better if she hadn't died quite so soon after her resurrection! It had been the sheerest chance that she'd been spotted at the West London Air Terminal and, having accustomed himself to the fact that she was still alive, Fast had made his further plans. It had been pretty clear to him that she must have known all the time where Burgoyne was...

And what about James Packard?

Was *he* dead—or not?

There hadn't been a smell of him since he'd gone into the stream but if there had been one miracle there could have been another. And that night, when they all met in his flat, Adam Fast's anxieties grew worse. Before the others arrived he had gone through every newspaper he could get his hands on. He'd read every single inch of those papers but there hadn't been a mention of a killing in a hotel. There had been a knifing down by the Naples docks—a seaman, believed to have started a drunken brawl—and an old man had been found dead in mysterious circumstances in a village outside the town. But there was nothing about any English girl.

Nothing at all. So what the hell could that possibly mean?

He asked the question of Cino shortly after seven-thirty. 'Do they just shrug this sort of thing off in Naples?' he asked crushingly. 'Do the chambermaids sweep them up with the empty cigarette packets—or what?' His full lower lip, red and fleshy, jutted dangerously.

Cino flapped his hands. His eyes were glassy, 'No—no, *Signore*. It is not like that. I am as disturbed as you.'

'You're going to be very considerably more disturbed soon, Cino, if you don't give me a good explanation. Did you dream the whole thing—or bungle it—fail to finish her off—or did you just make it all up on the spur of the moment to cover the fact you'd failed to find any information about Burgoyne? Well, Cino?'

'It was none of this,' Cino said desperately. 'She died, I know she died! I have no

150

possible shadow of a doubt about this.'

'*Then where is she?*'

'*Signore*, I cannot say!'

'I see. It seems to me,' Adam Fast said softly, 'that you have something more to tell us, Cino. Dead bodies don't vanish of their own accord, do they, Cino? It needs someone to do that for them, doesn't it, my friend?' He stared at the Italian for some seconds, watching him cringe, then he nodded at Rollo and Bearsted. 'Right,' he said. His lips worked and a flush came to his cheeks. 'I think we all know what to do, don't we?'

They knew well enough. Within less than half an hour Cino had been reduced to a blubbering wreck who whined for the beating-up to stop.

'Okay,' Fast said, drawing on his glowing cigarette.

'You talk, we stop. You don't talk, we go on. And on.' Once again he moved the cigarette close.

'I talk,' Cino screamed. The scream was muffled by a thick blanket so as not to disturb the neighbours, but it was a scream just the same, and the agony was real. Fast nodded at Rollo, who let the Italian go. Cino lay weeping for a few minutes then pulled himself to a sitting position on the floor. Through swollen lips he muttered, 'There is only one thing I did not tell you, *Signore*. Everything else I told you was true. I swear this. The girl was dead. I made no bungle, *Signore*. I—'

'What did you fail to tell me, Cino?' Once more the cigarette-end glowed red.

'No, no—I tell you!' Cino said in a high voice. He swallowed. 'There was a man.'

Fast's eyes flickered and his whole body tensed. 'A man? What man? Where?'

'I do not know what man. I did not get a good look at him. It was very sudden, *Signore*...it was at the bottom of the fire escape, as I was leaving.' He stared, from terrified eyes.

'Go on, Cino.'

'Yes, *Signore*. This man came at me from the shadows in the courtyard. All I can say is that he was tall. I knocked him out with a kick that landed, I think, in his face. He fell and I ran away.'

'Did you kill him too?' Fast asked ironically.

'This is unlikely, *Signore*. He would only have been knocked out.'

'You didn't wait to see?'

152

'No.'

'And he didn't come after you?'

Again Cino said, 'No. I got away and I was not seen again. And I was not seen before. Only by this man.'

'Only by this man,' Adam Fast repeated softly, his eyes glowing with a dangerous red fleck in the whites. 'And you don't know who this man was...and you haven't even wondered why *he* hasn't stirred something up, even though the body has disappeared?'

'No, *Signore*....I...'

'Well,' Fast said, 'I can tell you who he was. Or I'm pretty sure I can.' He looked at Rollo and Bearsted and his face was far from pleasant. 'How about you two?'

Rollo said, 'James Packard.'

Fast nodded. 'Precisely. And for reasons of his own James Packard has taken possession of the body and is keeping it hidden. I'd just like to know what those reasons are. I'm not specially interested in Miss Lois Chailey's corpse...but I'm very interested indeed in Mr James Packard! In the meantime we have one more potential problem: what to do to make another body disappear.'

Cino asked, 'Another body? Whose, *Signore?*'

Adam Fast laughed gently. He looked at his watch, then glanced at Rollo and gave a slight inclination of his head. Casually Rollo moved away, then came up behind Cino. A gun barrel slammed down on the Italian's head and he went down into Bearsted's arms. Bearsted lowered him to the floor without a sound. Fast said genially, 'Good—well done. Carry him to the car, please. We'll attend to this first and we'll see about Packard when we get back.'

They drove out of Naples in the general direction of Avellino, through a soft Mediterranean night and beneath a clear sky heavy with low-slung stars. They passed through the cultivation of the orange groves into wilder country that soon became hilly and, skirting Avellino on a road that was little more than a rutted, fearful track, they headed on through the hills towards Potenza. They were travelling at a high speed that seemed to shake the car to pieces. In a remote and lonely valley deep in the hillsides they stopped and they all got out and Cino, whimpering with terror, was held by Adam Fast and Bearsted while Rollo used the gun-barrel again and again until the skull fractured. Then Cino was stripped of any give-away possessions and artistically lain out in a cairn of small boulders, after which, without speaking, the men turned away and got back in the car and returned to Naples. Back in his flat Adam Fast called a local number on the telephone and fifteen minutes after that a tall, cadaverous Greek arrived.

Fast welcomed him and said, 'This morning, Ghiras, you told me the man Packard had not come to Italy.'

Ghiras nodded. 'This is true, yes. To the best of my knowledge he has not come.'

'Then you'd better get your knowledge up-to-date,' Fast said threateningly. 'I'm pretty sure he's right here in Naples. I want you to get the grapevine working overtime, Ghiras. I want all the hotels checked for everyone who's arrived in say the last week from Britain. I want the names and I want the descriptions. I want their contacts and their supposed reasons for coming here.'

'This will take time,' Ghiras said. 'It can and will be done—but it will take time.'

Fast said, 'Ghiras, my friend, it had better not take too much time because I'm in a big hurry. Remember, there's plenty of cash in this for you. And we're not so far off the jackpot. We just have to find this Packard and deal with him and then we're on the trail for Brett Burgoyne.'

Ghiras asked eagerly, 'Do you then know where he is?'

Fast smiled. 'No,' he said, 'I don't. But a certain person made a wise remark during the afternoon.' He told the Greek about Lois Chailey without mentioning what had happened subsequently to the Italian, Cino. 'That's another job for you and your grapevine, Ghiras. Put out the story that the girl's dead. When that piece of news reaches Burgoyne, then I reckon we've got him, because I know Burgoyne and I happen to know how he felt about Miss Lois Chailey.' He smiled again, his good humour completely restored together with his confidence. 'Like I told you, Ghiras, we're not so far off the jackpot.'

FOURTEEN

'I rather think,' Packard said as he came back onto the terrace where he had left Felicity, 'that the long, long waiting period is over.' It was three days now since Lois Chailey had died.

She looked up at him, shading her eyes from the sun. 'How's that?'

'The call,' he said, 'was a phony.' He'd been called to the telephone a few minutes earlier. 'Somebody's got rattled as I expected they would—and someone's got on to me. And I give you three guesses who.'

'Adam Fast?'

'Right. At least, he's the one I'd put my money on.'

'What did the man say on the phone?'

Packard laughed. 'That he'd picked up the word I was interested in Brett Burgoyne and if I would meet him in one hour's time outside a camera accessories shop in the Via Roma, he would sell me some information.'

'Was it Fast speaking, James?' She looked suddenly anxious.

He shook his head. 'It was an Italian. Fast wouldn't take that sort of risk. I'm to go alone—naturally. The police are not to be brought in—also naturally.'

'So?'

He grinned. 'So they're not going to be brought in—not too obviously, that is! I'd just like to take a look at that caller, without being seen myself.' He looked at his watch. 'I've got a call to make myself on the way down,' he said, 'so I'll start for the Via Roma right away. While I'm gone, I want you to go to your room and stay there, all right? You won't open the door to anybody, and make sure the windows are locked. I'll be asking the police to send a plain clothes man up here as well, just to keep an eye open. We don't want anything to happen to you.'

She asked, 'Think the call could be a decoy, just to get you away?'

'I'm not overlooking the possibility—let's put it that way. Scared?'

'Well, what do you think? Not too scared, though.' She smiled up at him, twisting a strand of hair around a finger. 'Look after yourself, James. Anything else you want me to do?'

He said, 'No, just keep behind locked doors, that's all.' He turned away. She watched him as he went quickly along the terrace; there was a wistful expression in her eyes as she did so, and an increase in her pulse. She didn't want anything to go wrong for him and it so easily could...but at least he was well aware that the call would be a phony. She shrugged off her fears, collected the magazines she had been leafing through, and obeyed orders by going up to her room right away.

From a telephone box *en route* for the town, Packard called police headquarters and spoke to the officer he had dealt with in connection with Lois Chailey's body. He said, 'I'm heading for the rendezvous now. I'm going to keep out of sight and just watch. I'd appreciate it if you'd send a plain clothes man up to the Hotel Anzio right away, to keep an eye on any developments that could impact on Miss Teal while I'm away—and send a detective with a good memory for faces to watch the Via Roma and see if he can spot anyone with a record.'

Malfa said, 'Very well, *Signore*, I shall come myself. I have news for you, as it happens, but this can wait until later.'

Packard thanked him and hung up.

It had happened all too swiftly, all too easily, not long after Packard had left that call-box. A wide-shouldered Italian sauntering up from the opposite direction on the other side of the road crossed casually towards Packard and spoke to him. To any disinterested bystander this man would have appeared to be doing no more than ask for a light, or a street direction. What he actually said, pleasantly enough and with a smile, was, 'Signor Packard, I have you covered. You will give no trouble, please.'

He had moved close now. Packard said, 'You're willing to use a gun in the street, are you, friend? It's not all that crowded, I know, but—'

'Not a gun, not here. A knife. At this moment it is aimed for your stomach. Death will be messy, but you will appear merely to be drunk meanwhile. Signor, along the road ahead there is a car, a blue Renault. You will get in, please, before I have to use the knife and carry you in. You understand?'

Packard's eyes flickered all around. As

he had said, there were not many people about; the ambush spot had been professionally selected. And that knife wouldn't miss. He shrugged and walked on. He had to play along with them. When he failed to turn up back at the hotel, Felicity would set the wheels moving. That was the one hope and it was a pretty slim one really, for she wouldn't have any leads at all as to where he'd been taken.

Nor, he suspected, would the police; because it began to seem to him unlikely that they would head for the Via Roma after all.

As he came abreast of the blue Renault the near-side rear door was pushed open and the knife, nudging into him now, pushed him towards it. There was another Italian waiting for him in the back and another man was in the driving seat all set to go. He got in, accompanied by the man who had picked him up and who now produced a small revolver. As soon as they were in, the car was driven away fast. And not towards the Via Roma either. No one spoke until Packard asked, 'Where are you taking me? The Sibley Boys' hide-out?'

'You will see.'

'I just like to know,' Packard murmured. 'It's just that I never was really keen on mystery trips.'

The man on his right nudged with his gun. 'Do not make jokes,' he said. 'No one laughs.'

'I'd try it sometime if I were you,' Packard suggested. After that he gave it up. The Renault was soon out of Naples and heading, though Packard couldn't know this, along the road that Cino had taken, out towards Avellino and beyond. But they didn't get that far. They were in fact not far out of town when the Italians got the message of the two police motor-cyclists roaring up behind.

At once consternation took over. So did mutual recrimination. Packard sat back, grinning and waiting his chance. He had no more idea than his escorts how the police had got on to them; but all that mattered was the fact that they had. The Renault's driver put his foot hard down and the car rocketed away. It had plenty of power, plenty of speed behind it. Where the motor-cyclists had been overtaking, they now fell behind—but only temporarily. They started after a while to surge ahead again and slowly they began to close the

Renault and then, a few minutes later, one of them came up alongside on the left.

The driver moved the wheel a fraction. The Renault swerved towards the racing policeman, who wasn't quite quick enough to take avoiding action. The car's left front wing took him and threw him. His machine smashed into the bodywork but the Renault straightened and roared on. Still the gun was being held against Packard's side and the man's eyes, steady and watchful as ever, said he would use it the moment he had to. Meanwhile the second motor-cyclist had slowed and turned around to do what he could for his companion. In the Renault the man on Packard's left said suddenly, 'They will be alerting Avellino by radio. Take the next turning right, Medinelli.'

The driver nodded and soon after that they made a screaming right-hand turn onto a poorly surfaced road. Packard bumped up and down, felt the rasp of the gun in his side and expected it to go off at any moment. The breakneck speed was kept up; farther along they crashed through a village, sending black-shawled old women, and livestock, beating it fast for safety. Fists shook in the air behind them. Then once again, distantly now, the motor-cycle was seen to be following, just the one man. And shortly after that, as they raced up towards an intersection ahead, they saw the police car turning into their path and coming for them fast.

Medinelli slammed on his brakes and with tyres screaming pulled the Renault round. Obviously, it was going to be easier to deal with the motor-cycle than the car and that man looked like riding to destruction. Medinelli put the front wheels into the soft earth of a field and for a happy moment it looked as if he might stick, but there was to be no such luck for he wrenched the Renault clear, put it back on the road, went fast and expertly through the gearbox and roared back the way they had come.

Now they were closing the motor-cyclist fast. Behind them the police car was just about holding its own. It was going to be a while before it could overtake or before a further interception could be made from ahead. In the meantime the motor-cycle policeman was going to hit bad trouble any second and Packard didn't want that to happen. If it could be avoided.

And he believed it could.

But it was going to be dead risky.

In the next split-second he moved very fast indeed. Using his hands, flat on the seat close to his knees, as a kind of springboard, he sent himself over the back of the front seat to land smack on the driver. Behind him a gun went off and something thudded into the upholstery and then shooting became an irrelevancy. The Renault slewed left violently, shot across on to the bare earth, rose on its side, came down again and then rolled right over onto its roof. There was a complete shambles inside and a man moaned. Blood was everywhere. From the engine in the rear came a lick of flame and as the police car and the motor-cycle pulled up and armed men ran towards the wreck, the flames spread rapidly.

At first Packard fancied his neck was broken, but it was no more than a pulled muscle. He had passed out and had come round in an ambulance, not a very comfortable one, and one of the policemen was inside with him. So was one of the Italians, who had also escaped lightly. This was the driver, who had probably been helped by being beneath Packard.

Packard asked about the others.

'Both dead,' the policeman answered. He didn't seem at all sorry.

How's your motor-cyclist, the one we hit?'

'Not badly hurt.'

'That's good,' Packard said. Then he asked, 'How did your people pick us up, anyway?'

'It was the purest chance, *Signore*. After you had telephoned, Signor Malfa was going to the Via Roma, where you had said, when he happened to see the blue Renault...and he recognised Alfredo Medinelli.'

'Uh-huh.' Packard was still feeling pretty dazed. 'And Medinelli meant something to him, did he?'

'*Si, Signore,*' the policeman said happily. 'Medinelli has been convicted many times in this country, of violence and of being involved with stolen cars. The Renault itself, I need hardly say, will be found to have been stolen and to have had its number changed.' The policeman, who was a sweaty man, wiped at his neck with a big handkerchief. 'But now Medinelli is wanted also in your own country, is this not so, Medinelli?'

'Find out for yourself,' the man snapped in Italian, his eyes hard and unsubdued.

Packard asked, 'For what—in Britain?'

'For a big robbery of diamonds from your London diamond area of Hatton Garden.'

FIFTEEN

'I don't get it,' Packard said at police headquarters. 'But just before you explain, *Signore*—is Miss Teal all right?'

The police chief nodded. 'Yes. I still have a man there, and will leave him as long as you wish, Signor Packard. Now to the explanation. As it happened, the report reached me only this morning via Interpol.'

'What report was that?'

'Why, that our old friend Medinelli was believed to have been concerned in your Hatton Garden diamond robbery, *Signore*. It appears that it was not known at the time that he was one of the men—I understand your London police believed all the men had been arrested—and this has become known since.'

'Known?' Packard asked. 'Is it definite that Medinelli was involved?'

'I gather not entirely known, no, but strongly suspected.'

Packard frowned and ran a hand over his jaw. 'Suspected of actual participation—or of being concerned at this end, say as a receiver?'

'Of actual participation.'

'How did they acquire this...hindsight information?'

'A detective of your Scotland Yard overheard some conversation in a bar.'

'I'd like to have a look at the report, if I may?'

'But certainly.' Malfa picked up a typewritten sheet of paper from his desk and passed it across to Packard. Packard read through it carefully but learned nothing further. The facts were just as the Italian had reported them and they were clear enough. But Packard was no less surprised than he had been when he had first heard the fresh information in the ambulance. True enough, there was nothing in the least unusual in the fact that information as such had come to hand after the trial; but it was certainly surprising that not one of the sentenced men had ever so much as mentioned the name of Medinelli. Such honour among thieves was, in his experience, certainly unusual. Unless, of course, Medinelli's security from arrest was in some way bound up with those men's fates—and financial arrangements—after their release.

But even so...

Packard put the document down on the policeman's desk and sat back in his chair, frowning up at the ceiling. He asked, 'What charge are you holding Medinelli on?'

Malfa shrugged. 'At the moment, obstructing the police and resisting arrest.'

'And injuring one of your men?'

'This is being considered. We have not formulated the charge until we consult our lawyers.'

'What about this Interpol business? Is Medinelli to be extradited?'

'This will also have to be considered, but at a higher level, of course.'

'Have you reported back that you've got him?'

'Not that we have got him, there has not been time. I have reported, this morning,

that we would be taking steps to arrest
him, yes.'

'I see. *Signore,* I wonder if you would
allow me to question Medinelli myself?'

The policeman pursed his lips, then
shrugged. 'I think this will be possible,
yes. I see no reason to refuse, in the
circumstances. When do you wish to do
this?'

Packard said, 'Right away, if possible,
Signor Malfa. Could you have him sent
for now?'

'Yes.' The policeman pressed a switch
in the intercom on his desk and spoke to
a secretary. Within two minutes Medinelli
was brought in by two men. Malfa told
these men to wait outside, then nodded
at Packard. 'Please proceed,' he said.

Packard sat back comfortably and looked
at Medinelli over clasped hands. He asked,
'You have been informed, I take it, of why
you were wanted by the police?'

Medinelli scowled and turned to the
man behind the desk.

'I do not have to answer this man,' he
said in Italian. 'Who is he?'

'He has my authority and you will
answer his questions.'

Packard said, 'Thank you, *Signore.*' He

smiled. 'And he knows perfectly well who I am. Don't you, Medinelli?'

'I do not know anything about you,' Medinelli answered in English.

'Really? Then why were you so anxious to get hold of me?'

'I was not anxious,' the man said off-handedly.

'You were just obeying orders?'

There was no answer.

'Adam Fast's orders...or Rollo's?'

'I have never heard of these people.'

Packard smiled, icily. 'You expect me to believe that? Come, come, Signor Medinelli! I know far better than that. You'd been hired by Adam Fast to take part in an attempt to kidnap me and, no doubt, murder me. You may as well admit it, because it's not going to be at all difficult to prove it.'

'I have nothing to say.'

Packard shrugged. 'Very well, have it your own way for now. But you do know Brett Burgoyne, don't you?'

A curious flicker passed across Medinelli's face for a moment, then he was as stony as ever. 'I have never heard of him either,' he said.

171

'I see. You've been in London, of course.'

'I had nothing to do with the robbery,' Medinelli said.

'Well, time will tell as to that, but that wasn't what I was referring to. You have, in fact, visited Britain?'

'That is true,' Medinelli said after a pause. 'I have visited London, yes.'

'When?'

He shrugged. 'Oh, a number of times.'

'When was the last time?'

'About a year ago...perhaps a little more.'

'How long have you been in Britain altogether?'

'I don't know.'

'Try and think, Medinelli.'

The man licked his lips. 'It is hard to say...maybe it'd all add up to around six to eight months.'

'I congratulate you, Medinelli.'

He stared. 'On what?'

'Your English. It's terribly good. Why do you answer in English, by the way?'

'You used English. It was a courtesy —nothing more.'

Packard's eyes flickered. 'A courtesy, eh? Tell me—what was the real purpose of your visits to London?'

'Purely personal reasons.'

'Oh, come now! Don't forget what the London police want to see you about, Medinelli.'

'I've already said—'

'I know what you've said, just answer the question, please. What did you go to London for, Medinelli?'

'I like London,' Medinelli snapped. He was sweating now. 'I go for a holiday when I can get away. Nothing else.'

Packard shrugged. 'Right, that's your story and you're sticking to it. For now. Believe you me, Medinelli, it's going to peel to pieces before long.' He lit a cigarette and while he did so he asked casually, 'I suppose you know your pal Adam Fast was responsible for Lois Chailey being strangled?'

He was watching carefully but Medinelli gave nothing away beyond a curious tightening of the flesh around his eyes—and there was a faint tremor in his voice when he said, 'I don't know what you're talking about.'

'You don't know Adam Fast?'

'I've said so, haven't I, for Christ's sake?'

173

Packard raised his eyebrows. 'Or Lois Chailey?'

'I don't know her either.'

'I see.' Slowly, Packard got to his feet, stretched, and went up close to Medinelli. Suddenly his left fist jabbed hard, smashingly, into the man's nose. Medinelli yelped, staggered back. Blood ran down his face and chin. He came in with his head low and Packard gave him another jab that sent him reeling back to collapse in a corner. Grinning, Packard winked at the police chief, who had got up from his desk looking highly astonished to say the least of it. Packard took a handkerchief from his pocket and went over to Medinelli. He mopped up the blood and stuffed the handkerchief back in his pocket. He said, 'I shouldn't have done that, of course. I'm sorry.' He turned to Malfa. 'All right,' he said, 'I've done with him. The sooner you have him removed, the better.'

'I think so too,' the policeman said stiffly. He was clearly startled and angry. Such a scene was going to look very bad when it came out in court. Brutality by the police was always to be deplored...he called out sharply and the two men came

174

back and removed Medinelli, who was already threatening to lift the roof off police headquarters via his lawyer.

When he had gone Packard said, 'I'm sorry about that, but it was necessary.'

'To show spleen, *Signore?*'

'No,' Packard said quietly, and brought out his handkerchief again, briefly. 'To get a blood sample without Medinelli realising what I was doing. You see, I have a theory. Or rather, let's just call it a hunch. It may be as screwy as a nut cake and just for now I'd rather not say any more—even to you. But I've got some investigating to do and until I've done it I'm going to ask you to hang on to Medinelli. Make sure his lawyer isn't allowed to spring him, and delay any moves towards extradition. This may take me a couple of days, but I'll work just as fast as I can and I'll contact you the moment I'm ready.'

'I've got a job for you,' Packard said back at the hotel. 'I want you to go to London right away and take something to the Scotland Yard laboratory in Theobalds Road, Holborn.'

Felicity grimaced. 'Why me? Don't I see enough of London, James? I'm enjoying life here, at least I am when I'm not shut up in my bedroom. Can't you go?'

'I'm not leaving you here alone, my darling, so just pipe down and listen. I want you to see a Dr Morgan and give him this.' He brought out the bloody handkerchief. 'I'll give you a letter for him as well. And when I said right away I meant just that, so start getting an overnight bag packed, will you?'

By this time the news of the kidnap fiasco had reached the flat in the Naples suburbs and Adam Fast was packing up. Rollo and Bearsted were with him and none of them was happy. Rollo in particular was badly on edge and had been hitting the bottle again. He kept saying, 'It's no bloody use, we've had it. That bastard Medinelli's going to talk.'

Fast rounded on him. 'Belt up,' he snarled. 'Sure he *could* talk, which is why we're moving out—isn't it? But he won't. Not if he knows what's good for him. And he does.' Even to himself it sounded hollow.

'They'll make him.'

'You know as well as I do, the cops in any country except maybe Russia don't risk using the sort of methods *we've* got used to. Short of that, Medinelli won't talk.'

'Jesus, I hope you're right.' Rollo sweated. 'What are we going to do in Rome, anyway?'

'Get lost for a while.'

'And Packard—and Burgoyne, and the—'

'It's going to have to wait, isn't it?' Fast pushed his face close to Rollo's, threateningly. 'You just shut your trap and do what I tell you.' He stepped back, simmered down. He said, 'Tell you something else.'

'Well?'

'We can't get out of town, not just yet. The heat's full on—bound to be. They'll know Medinelli wasn't on his own. There'll be road blocks everywhere. Same with the trains, they'll all be searched. We have to let it all die down a bit, that's all. Give it a few days, then we can try it on, but not just now.'

'So where do we go in the meantime —eh?'

'Live rough,' Fast told him. 'You can get out of those clothes for a start. We stop washing and shaving and we mix in with the riff raff. There's plenty of that in Naples—thank God!'

SIXTEEN

Felicity booked on the next flight out of Naples for London and from the airport she took the airline bus to the terminal and then a taxi. It was a filthy wet day, with the streets damp and depressing and the crowds of people more so, looking sick to death of the climate and the never-ending austerity and the financial crises that hit them every month with unfailing regularity. She wondered why they all stood for it when there was so much space and sun and laughter in other parts of the world. She couldn't care less, herself, if she never saw London ever again.

At the Theobalds Road laboratory she produced her CWA authority and asked to see Dr Morgan urgently. She hadn't long to wait; CWA's reputation had a happy way of cutting through any red tape that might be around. She was taken to Morgan's office. Harold Morgan was a tall, thin man in the middle thirties, wearing thick glasses and a white coat spotted with chemical stains.

He took the packet and the letter. He read through what Packard had written, then said, 'Ah-ha. Yes. I see. I think I can do this, but it may take a little time because there's—ah—something I have to get hold of before I can make the tests Mr Packard has asked for.'

She asked directly, 'What are those tests, Dr Morgan?'

He pursed his lips and fiddled with the letter, then peered at her short-sightedly and smiled. 'I'm sorry, but he's asked me not to say anything at this stage.'

'Oh,' she said, and her lips tightened. 'How long *is* all this going to take?'

Morgan said, 'Well now, that depends. I wouldn't expect to be ready until perhaps tomorrow.'

'Oh—I see,' she said rather blankly. It may have been stupid, but somehow she had been expecting to be on the plane for Naples again before then. 'Well—will you contact me, or do I...just come back tomorrow?'

Morgan said, 'If you'll leave me a telephone number, I'll ring.'

So she gave him her number and went

179

rather dismally home and in the end she did nothing, just stayed in her flat and went to bed early. Morgan's call came through at 1130 next morning and she went out and took a taxi to Theobalds Road and soon she was once again sitting in Morgan's office.

Morgan adjusted his spectacles and said carefully. 'James wanted a blood test made. A comparison, in fact—two tests. You see, as James evidently knew, an advance has been made in forensic science. Two of our Scotland Yard biologists have found a method of identifying bloodstains found on clothing and so on. They have discovered that proteins and enzymes—which are two of the basic ingredients of blood—have certain recognisable characteristics in each individual. Such characteristics are permanent and ineradicable—from the cradle to the grave as you might say. Now, in the first instance, the characteristics can be separated into—ah—broadish groups, categories, in very much the same way as a person's hair can be allocated into various colour-groupings. And in addition—and most important to us, Miss Teal—is the fact that the blood-proteins have characteristics that differ in every individual—they are never the same in any two persons—'

'Like fingerprints?'

Morgan nodded delightedly. 'Yes, Miss Teal—exactly—you have it! Now, all this is very exciting. We've even got ahead of ourselves—this wasn't expected to be available for some years yet, but in point of fact we are already making these tests on a limited scale. James knew this, of course, and knew that we haven't yet made this service available to all police forces, which is no doubt why he was wary of saying too much. However—as you so rightly said—the comparison is with fingerprints. A spot of blood has exactly the same story to tell as a fingerprint. And our discovery now sub-divides blood into a big range of brand-new groupings—we are no longer restricted to the old categories of ABO, MM and rhesus. And, d'you see, as a result of my having been supplied on request, following James's letter, with blood samples from the diamond robbery at Hatton Garden, I am able to tell you that his assumption is absolutely correct.'

Felicity asked, 'What assumption, Dr Morgan?'

He looked astonished for a moment,

raising his eyebrows, then apologised. 'Of course, you didn't know. The man Medinelli in Naples and the criminal Brett Burgoyne who escaped from where was it—Wandsworth prison—are one and the same person.'

'But how, how, how,' she asked Packard, when she was, thankfully, back in the sunshine, 'can they *possibly* be the same person?'

Packard grinned. 'Possible or not,' he said annoyingly, 'the fact remains—they are! Morgan's tests just cannot lie. Didn't he tell you that?'

'Oh, *yes*,' she said, wriggling her shoulders in exasperation. 'He said he was quite positive. But I still don't see how. I mean...if Burgoyne was in prison, which we know he was...and anyway, surely Adam Fast would have *known?*'

Packard said, 'Let's take the first point first, shall we? Sure, Brett Burgoyne was in prison, so what? So nothing! Maybe someone here in Italy missed Medinelli for a while—a girl-friend, or a business acquaintance, say. Once he was out, he'd have resumed the Medinelli role from time to time, maybe with the aid of a disguise.

Like me currently. Now let's take Adam Fast—'

'Yes,' she interrupted witheringly, 'lets! A facial would never have fooled anyone who knew Burgoyne intimately.'

'Agreed,' Packard said with weary and heavy patience. 'But don't you see, that's the point? We've absolutely no shred of evidence to suggest Fast *did* know Burgoyne intimately. Or even at all, in the personal sense. He could have been just a name—a dirty name, true, but still just a name. Burgoyne was never one of the Sibley Boys. He was just one of the mob that did Hatton Garden—and we've learned that the Sibley Boys only came into that indirectly, right? Just as the insurers, kind of.'

Felicity said, 'Well, yes, I suppose that does make sense, but if all that's true, why the hell, may I ask, did Burgoyne/Medinelli go and put himself right into the enemy camp like he did? He couldn't have been closer to the man who had come to get him, could he? So why?'

Packard grinned. 'Ever hear of the Trojan horse?' he asked. 'I don't say that was the idea, but it's all I can think of and it's quite logical really and I'd be prepared to take any bet I'm right.'

She looked at him critically, searchingly. 'I'm not going to argue,' she said. 'I've known you be right too often. But if you *are* wrong, don't mind me saying I told you so. By the way,' she added, 'how did you get this idea about Medinelli's identity in the first place, James?'

He said, 'Well, I'll admit he wasn't *too* unlike the photographs I'd seen of Burgoyne, though in fact I didn't tick over on that right away, as I said. Then, you see, Burgoyne was said to be able to pass as an Italian very convincingly. Medinelli had good command of English, which he used in a more idiomatic way now and again than I'd have expected from an Italian who'd only paid brief visits to England—which was what he tried to tell me. Okay?'

She made a face. 'Very, very erudite.'

He said, 'Dammit, you still don't really believe me *or* Morgan, do you?'

'No,' she said, 'not really. And I suppose that's a dangerous thing to say, too. Scientists have that much in common with you. Usually.'

He lifted an eyebrow. She explained, 'They're usually right. Or think they are. And find reasons to explain that they

184

were really, even after they've been proved wrong. If you follow.'

'I don't,' he said, 'but never mind.' He reached out a hand to her and his tone changed. 'Tired?' he asked.

'Yes,' she admitted. 'I've done a fair amount of travelling the last twenty-four hours. Are we on the trail again tonight?'

He was silent for a while then he said, 'As a matter of fact, no. It's latish. Medinelli will keep till morning, and the Fast mob won't get out of Naples. I've other plans.'

'What?' she asked a little breathlessly.

He said, 'First of all a good dinner somewhere nice, and then...' He didn't finish what he had been going to say and he knew there was no need to. She was responding to his touch and her hand was moving on his body and he knew from the way her lips were parting that their thoughts had met along the line and that it was going to be a wonderful night.

They woke late and Packard rolled over and kissed her on the lips. Then he got up and drew the curtains. It was a brilliant day. Sunlight sparkled on the deep blue water of the Tyrrhenian Sea, lifted brilliant colouring from Capri. Naples was white and brown below the heights, and in spite of the climbing sun there was a freshness in the air. Felicity got out of bed and joined him at the window, looking down with delight. It was a lot different from London, from Kensington and the City and the rushed snack lunches and the tubes and buses and queues. It would do her for the rest of her life. Especially after last night...

Packard looked down at her and drew her sun-browned body close to his own, felt again the thrill of flesh meeting. Then he broke the spell.

'Work,' he said abruptly.

'Well,' she said, 'that *is* what we're here for, after all. I suppose!'

'And we'll move in that direction before the chambermaid comes in,' he said with a smile. He kissed her again, on her face, on her honeygold hair, on her breasts. 'We don't want to shatter the good woman's illusions about the British.' He dressed quickly and went along to his own room, where he bathed and shaved and rang down for breakfast and then he collected Felicity and together they walked in the clear sunshine down to police headquarters.

Signor Malfa was glad enough to see them. He said, 'There is some difficulty in holding Medinelli.'

'Burgoyne,' Packard said.

'No, Medinelli,' Malfa said irritably. 'I—'

'I have something very interesting to tell you,' Packard interrupted. He explained everything in detail, dealing, as he had in Felicity's case, with the apparent objections. He added, 'I'm entirely satisfied there's no possible doubt about the identification. Now, Signor Malfa, tell me—what are these difficulties about holding Medinelli?'

Malfa shrugged. 'To me they do not hold water, but I need not perhaps tell you what lawyers are like—'

'Especially bent lawyers?'

'Yes, and even more especially bent ones from Rome who happen to have important contacts. It is going to be very, very difficult to continue holding this man for long, Signor Packard.'

'Okay, then,' Packard said indifferently. 'Let him go.'

Malfa bristled. 'Let him go—when he has run down one of our men?'

Packard said, 'Oh, he won't be gone for

long, I assure you! And when we catch up with him again, no lawyer in the world will ever spring him, not even if that lawyer is bent right in a circle. As a matter of fact, I was going to ask you to let him go temporarily in any case. Now his lawyers have come up with difficulties which make it hard to hold him—well, it's even better. He'll never suspect a thing—and of course he has no idea we've identified him as Brett Burgoyne. He'll feel one hundred per cent secure on that one. And he'll find his way back to Adam Fast, too. He'll do that because he'll still want to level the score.'

'The score, *Signore?*'

'Yes. don't you see? One of the reasons I began to suspect Medinelli and Burgoyne might be one and the same, was the way he reacted when I mentioned the strangling of Lois Chailey. His girl, Signor Malfa! He did his best, but he couldn't quite conceal his depth of feeling. And that's the score he's going to try to get level when he sees the chance. As soon as he feels it won't compromise him in any way, he's going to get Adam Fast and anyone else concerned. All we need to do is, let Medinelli go—and then tail him.'

SEVENTEEN

Medinelli was pretty happy at the way things had turned out. Sneering, too. He was a nasty piece of work, Packard thought. Lois Chailey had been much too good for him; but maybe he had some hidden virtues somewhere. At any rate Packard believed he'd genuinely loved the girl and that he had a real yen for revenge—personal revenge, so long as he himself was in the clear. To have turned Adam Fast in while he was himself in custody wouldn't have been in line with his plans at all.

Malfa said, before Medinelli's departure, which was to be discreetly shadowed by one of the plain clothes men from headquarters, 'I am wondering, Signor Packard, how much he will be suspecting a police tail.'

'Of course he'll be expecting it,' Packard said. 'He didn't come down with the last shower, after all. But he doesn't know we've got on to his identity and that's the really important thing. He's not exactly going to rush into anything, because of the tail—but as soon as he reckons he's thrown us off, he'll go right for Adam Fast. And he knows he won't have all that much time since he's still got the charges hanging over him—so my guess is, we won't have all that long to wait. In the meantime, we have to play this very, very gently, Signor Malfa, and I'm keeping right out of it until you report he's linked up with Adam Fast. Okay?'

Malfa shrugged. '*Signore,* one can only hope so. That is all. Undoubtedly we are sticking out our necks a very long way, in letting this Burgoyne go free...it was a stroke of luck that we should have got him at all, and now we throw away this luck! It is going to look very bad for me, *Signore,* to have released a man who is wanted by Interpol.'

Packard smiled. 'Sure we're sticking our necks out,' he agreed, 'but I've a feeling it's all going to work out the way we want it. Going back to what I was saying...about playing this thing gently. We have to play it clever too. So we do it this way—with your agreement, of course, Signor Malfa: we assume Medinelli's going to spot that tail, right? Well, I want a tail on the tail, a man with orders to spot Medinelli's reactions to Tail Number One. As soon as it appears to him that Medinelli's tumbled, he radios headquarters and a third man takes over. And so on and so on. Then as soon as it seems reasonable to do so, we put out a leak—I'm sure you have channels for such things—a leak that we've lost Medinelli. If that leak reaches Adam Fast too, so much the better. Then we'll have both parties trying to contact each other. And in the meantime, why not look on the bright side? You said yourself you were having difficulty with Medinelli's mouthpiece. Maybe you couldn't have held him much longer anyway.'

The Italian threw up his hands. 'Lawyers!' he said in a withering tone. 'I spit.' Plainly he didn't like to think of that mouthpiece getting away with it even temporarily. And equally clearly, the whole resources of the Naples police were going to be put behind the job of seeing to it that Medinelli hadn't a ghost of a chance of getting away with anything more. Which was just as Packard wanted it.

Medinelli had spotted that tail in the first fifteen minutes. As Packard had suggested, he knew there would be one; it took him the fifteen minutes to make the positive identification. And then he made a mistake: he decided not to make it too obvious that he'd spotted the man and he played him along for another half an hour before shaking him off—which gave the second man time to make his report and fix the shift-over. Medinelli, smirking to himself as he slid down a smelly back alley, took quite a while to tick over that he'd been picked up again and this time he made a much faster job of the shaking off procedure.

And he did it successfully. And with finality. There was no more tailing. When Malfa reported this on the telephone, frenziedly, to Packard, Packard simply didn't believe it. He thought it must be part of the pre-arranged leak, a phone call that, if by any chance overheard, would lend a little more authenticity to the leak itself. Malfa said beseechingly, 'Please, please, Signor Packard, come at once to my office!'

And there belief came. And blame as well. After all, it had been Packard's idea from the start. Packard took his share of the blame philosophically and asked, 'Well, what do you propose to do now, Signor Malfa?'

Malfa's mouth was hard, like a very thin line, the lips white in a white face. 'Naples is a big place,' he said, 'and very full of many people. But Medinelli is not going to get away. Already I have alerted all my men, both plain clothes and uniformed, to watch for Medinelli and arrest him on sight. All exits from the city—road, rail, sea, air—are being watched. He will be found. But not by your methods.'

'Fine,' Packard said dourly, 'up to a point, *Signore*. I agree he has to be spotted. But, for the moment, no more than that.'

Malfa danced up and down. 'But—'

'Just a minute,' Packard said. 'I still have to get Adam Fast and I have still to bring in all the others as well. It's part of the job. By all means have Medinelli watched for and go on watching the exits—I'm all in favour—but please don't make any arrests unless you can get them all together. That's important. I—'

'You speak of murders. *Signore*, if I arrest Medinelli, he will not be able to murder anybody!'

'Sure, I know that.' Packard sighed. 'But it still leaves Adam Fast at large, doesn't it? Believe me, it's very important that we wrap up his organisation for good and all.

He's a killer, you know.'

'He has not broken the law here, he has not been asked for by Interpol, he—'

'Not yet, but he will be,' Packard assured him. 'And even though he may not have broken your laws directly, he was behind Medinelli, and that girl's death—as you very well know. Signor Malfa, we still have to go gently on this. Once you've identified Medinelli again, we just have to make damn sure he doesn't get lost again. That's all. It shouldn't be too difficult, not with the whole force on the job...'

It took time but in the end Packard made his point. But he shuddered to think what would happen if Medinelli/Burgoyne did slip through the net again.

'I do hope,' Adam Fast said casually, but with ice behind it, 'that you didn't open your trap, Medinelli?'

'What do *you* think?' Medinelli answered surlily. 'I didn't say a thing that could incriminate me or maybe I wouldn't have found it so easy to get out...and this meant not incriminating you either, *Signore.*'

'Okay,' Fast said. His fleshy cheeks wobbled into a smile. 'Frankly, I'm surprised you did get away, Medinelli

194

—after injuring a policeman.'

'It was accidental.'

'The man is still knocked up,' Fast said smoothly. He rasped at his cheeks; they were stubbly and dirty. The same applied to Rollo and Bearsted. They were sleazy and tattered and more-or-less hungry but the disguise was good and it held. They had inhabited the back alleys ever since they had left the flat in the suburbs, sleeping as best they could in dark doorways or up stinking passages alive with rats and heavy with the aroma of assorted garbage. Fast had had quite enough of it; he said angrily, 'You don't imagine they aren't watching you, do you?'

'No. There was a tail. I shook it off.'

Fast nodded. 'Yes, I accept you did that, you're not a fool.' They had met Medinelli, after word had reached them through the underground network organised by the Greek, Ghiras, that he was free, in a back-alley café where they sunk into the background nicely among many others of the nomadic sector of the Naples population. Medinelli wouldn't have made that rendezvous if he hadn't been certain he had shaken off any tail. Unless, that was, the police were making use of him...which was a thought that had certainly entered Fast's mind but which he preferred to keep to himself for the time being. He wasn't taking the thought too seriously, for there was no reason actually to distrust Medinelli, and he and his companions were well enough armed to deal nicely with any police ambush, especially in an area where the police didn't have too many friends. Fast went on, 'All the same, you're a risk from now on out, aren't you, Medinelli?'

Medinelli shook his head. 'I'm not so sure of that, *Signore*. They let me go of their own free will—'

'Assisted by that mouthpiece, Medinelli.'

Medinelli shrugged, and spoke as though trying to convince himself as much as anyone else. 'True, but if they had been able to keep me, they would have done so. There can be nothing fresh to make them arrest me now.'

Fast pursed his lips. 'Time will tell,' he said. 'Meanwhile we should not be too much in each other's company. And there's something else, Medinelli.'

'Yes?'

'Yes,' Fast said in a soft voice. 'Something I have not yet mentioned, but it's none the less on my mind. Medinelli...you didn't get Packard, did you? You let him get you.'

Medinelli avoided his eye.

'That's not what I expect, Medinelli. It will never occur again. I think you understand me—don't you?'

Medinelli did. But there was a curious twist to his lips when he said so. Fast went on more crisply, 'Well, I'll leave it at that—for now. The future is of more concern to me just at the moment. You got any suggestions, Rollo?'

Rollo swallowed some coffee and said, 'Yes, as a matter of fact I have. I don't like this...I mean, having Medinelli around. In the circumstances, see?'

Fast nodded. 'Yes, I do see. I had to have his report of the proceedings—you know that—but now...yes, I see what you mean. I was thinking precisely the same, Rollo.'

Rollo lifted an eyebrow. 'Out?' he asked.

'Out, Rollo. And quick. So far, the heat's not on us. We need to take advantage of that, in my opinion.' He shifted on the hard stool provided by the café. 'I want to get back to civilisation, which is also important. In Rome we'll be comfortable—and safe. Very safe.'

Bearsted said mournfully, 'Yes, if we can get there.'

'We'll get there all right. But not together.'

'Not together?' Rollo looked at him. 'You mean—not with Medinelli?'

'Correct. I'm sorry, Medinelli. I'm sure you understand, though. You know the address in Rome. You'll make your own way there. But not at once. Not until the day after tomorrow, Medinelli. And not direct either. You'll keep on remembering they'll be watching you. Can you cope?'

'But certainly,' Medinelli said. He was quite confident. 'This is my country, I know its ways, I know the police. If they find me at all, they certainly won't have me in sight for very long!'

'Good,' Fast said easily. 'Just so long as you don't come anywhere near that address until you're dead certain you've shaken them off. And now I think you'd better leave us. Good luck, Medinelli.'

After Medinelli had gone Rollo asked, 'When do *we* go, then?'

'Tonight—while we're still in the clear. But not to Rome. To Taranto.'

Rollo stared. *'Taranto?* Then why tell—'

'Medinelli?' Fast laid a hand on his arm

and said gently, 'My dear Rollo, Medinelli may easily be re-arrested. It's better that he doesn't know. Pressure could be applied, you know. And after all...Medinelli is expendable, isn't he?'

'I suppose so, yes.' He added, 'How do we go?'

Promply Fast said, 'By train. Granted the stations may be watched for Medinelli—I wouldn't know, it all depends why they released him—but they're not looking for us and they don't know anything about us so they won't recognise us or bother us.'

'Why not by road?'

Fast said irritably, 'If you think anyone's going to hire out a car to us looking the way we do, you're crazy. And I'm not risking knocking one off just at the moment. You needn't worry. We'll be absolutely okay by train, and I know exactly where to go in Taranto.'

'What about Burgoyne?' Rollo asked pointed. 'You haven't forgotten we're looking for him, have you?'

'No, I haven't forgotten, Rollo.'

Three hours after Medinelli had left Adam Fast and the others a policeman picked him up and radioed a report to headquarters. At once an urgent call went out. There was still no tail as such but from then on, unknowingly, Medinelli was passed on from one uniformed man to another and at 1600 hours the telephone in the Hotel Anzio brought Packard down to see Malfa urgently.

Malfa came straight to the point. He said, 'At 1550 hours Medinelli was seen to buy a rail ticket.'

'Where for?'

'Enquiries revealed that this ticket was for Rome.'

'And he caught a train?'

'No. He had left the station by a street exit. With the new timetables there is no train for Rome for another two hours. What do you wish us to do, Signor Packard?'

'Keep on watch, please. Don't lose him, and make damn sure he's watched right through till he catches that train. I'll stay here meantime, if I may. And as soon as he's seen moving for the station, I want to know. I'll be catching that train myself. It rather looks as though Adam Fast didn't hang around and wait for Medinelli, doesn't it? For my money, he'll be found in Rome.'

EIGHTEEN

Inside Brett Burgoyne's heart there was that cold knot of hate that had been with him ever since he had learned of Lois Chailey's death and who had been responsible for it. It was this that had made him join up with Adam Fast once again—he had worked for Fast before in Italy—strictly in his role as Luigi Medinelli—and Fast trusted him. Fast had been glad to have his help this time, all right—at least until he had failed to finish off James Packard. And Burgoyne was going to get Adam Fast for sure, now.

There had been something in Fast's manner that day that had suggested to Burgoyne that the fat man had had no intention of heading for Rome. That had been a red herring because he, Burgoyne—or in this context, Medinelli —was in fact no longer trusted or regarded as a safe bet since he had been in police hands. If that was the way Fast was looking at it, it was of course from his point of view entirely natural and reasonable, but Burgoyne had his other ideas and because of those other ideas he returned to the railway station after a while and sat unobtrusively in the crowds with his head sunk in a newspaper, waiting and watching.

And in due course he was rewarded.

'What's the idea, I wonder?' Packard frowned. He had been waiting with Malfa for some while now in the stationmaster's office. Burgoyne had made no attempt to join the queue for the Rome train, which in the event had pulled away without him; and he had sat on into the evening behind his paper, anonymous still—except to the hidden watchers—and unobtrusive.

'Why buy a ticket to Rome if you're not going to use it?'

Malfa said, 'Perhaps he is waiting for this Adam Fast.'

'It's very unlikely, I think. I wouldn't have thought he'd be sitting around in the open like that, and in any case I still believe Fast will have gone ahead. Somehow, this doesn't quite add up.' He looked out of the window, saw Burgoyne still there. He studied the man through binoculars, tried to interpret the expression on the face whenever the newspaper gave him the chance to do so. It didn't really help much. Burgoyne looked anxious and watchful and that was about all one could make of it. He was looking at everyone who came in through the booking hall towards the departure platforms and it was certainly clear that he was expecting somebody. Who, was a matter for sheer guesswork now.

Packard lowered the glasses and put them down on a table and lit a cigarette and then suddenly Malfa grabbed at his arm and said excitedly, 'Look, *Signore*, look!'

Packard looked. Burgoyne/Medinelli was getting up, folding his newspaper. He had done this twice before, once to buy some chocolate and cigarettes, once to go to the gents. This time his movements seemed to have a little more purpose and his eyes were bright and more watchful—as though this time they were focused on something positive.

Then he moved out of sight.

Malfa picked up a microphone and spoke into it, briefly. Thirty seconds later a report came through to him and he said to Packard, 'Medinelli is buying another rail ticket, *Signore*. For Taranto.'

'*Taranto?* So that's it—Rome was just a blind.' Packard swung round on the stationmaster. 'When does the next train leave for Taranto?'

'In seven minutes, *Signore*.'

'Right! Signor Malfa, is there anyone else with Medinelli now?'

Malfa held up a hand. 'There is a report coming...no, *Signore*, he is alone still,' he said after a moment. 'Now he is going away from the ticket office...not yet towards the Taranto train.'

'Let's hope your men don't lose him —this could be another unused ticket for all we know.'

Malfa said, 'They will not lose him now, *Signore*, you need not worry.' He listened to his transistorised two-way radio. 'Still the man is alone and he is looking at the magazines on a bookstall now. He seems to be in no hurry. Now he is buying a magazine.' There was a pause. 'It seems he is a man who catches trains at the very last moment, *Signore*.'

'Still alone, is he?'

'Still alone, yes. Ah—now he is leaving the book-stall. He is going towards the platform for Taranto, in a moment we shall see him, but only distantly.' There was another pause. 'He is now at the barrier, Signor Packard, and he is still alone. As you can perhaps see, there are few people going through just now.'

Packard, watching through his binoculars, nodded. He could see Burgoyne now, and those few other people. There was no one else he recognised...he could no doubt have the train held and searched in case Burgoyne had friends aboard, but that could lead to a lost contact if none were found, for Burgoyne wouldn't be of any further use once the authorities had shown their hand. Packard lowered the binoculars and said, 'Right—you know what to do, Signor Malfa. We just have to hope nothing goes wrong now.' He picked up a two-way transistor, a much smaller one than Malfa's, a mere disc which he pinned behind the lapel of his jacket, then he turned to the stationmaster. 'All ready,' he said. He looked at the clock on the wall. 'Three minutes to go. I'll time myself to board the trains as near as possible on the dot, and I want you to send her off the moment I get on, all right?'

'All right, yes, *Signore*—'

'And the ticket. I don't want to get pinched for bumming a free ride!'

The official smiled and handed Packard his ticket for Taranto. 'It was made out as soon as Signor Malfa mentioned the new destination,' he said. 'Good luck, *Signore*.'

'Thank you.' Packard left the station-master's room and walked out towards the Taranto train. One or two stragglers were going through to the platform and the train was ready to be signalled away. Watching the time closely Packard stopped to buy a newspaper, then moved for the train. A few seconds after the departure time he went through to the platform, running now as though to beat the clock, and as he scrambled aboard the rear coach a plain clothes man had an attack of coughing and spoke briefly into a microphone concealed in the palm of his hand. In the stationmaster's room Malfa nodded and the stationmaster said one word into the telephone whose line had been waiting open since Packard left the room.

The Taranto express pulled smoothly away and gathered speed quickly.

Burgoyne thought triumphantly: Stage

One over and neatly done. He sneered a little; they weren't as clever as they thought they were—and 'they' covered the police as well as Adam Fast. Maybe the police wouldn't have been expecting him to show up at any such place as a railway station; quite often in his life he had found that to do the obvious was the safest thing. The police mind moved in grooves and they seldom saw what was rammed under their noses. Nevertheless, he had to acknowledge the element of luck and he admitted too that under normal circumstances he just might not have risked it at all. But he had to get Adam Fast—that was the primary consideration now. And even if they had happened to spot him, the police would probably not have re-arrested him. They couldn't, not unless they'd found something new to go on, and it would have to be good to get past his mouthpiece. If they ever tumbled to the fact that he'd headed out for Taranto he could, of course, expect the Taranto police to be alerted to watch him—and he would have to accept that. And after he had dealt with Fast it would be up to him to make himself very, very scarce. He ought to be able to knock off a boat in Taranto, and head across, say, to North Africa. That was big enough to hide him for a while and from there he could transact his financial business and get the cash transferred without too much trouble. He had quite enough to pay well for services rendered and these days money didn't just talk, it shouted its orders loud and clear and plenty of officials were ready to jump and obey.

He slid a hand into a pocket and fingered the knife that he was going to use on Adam Fast and Rollo and Bearsted. He smiled inwardly. If only they knew he was on the train with them...but they didn't, because he'd been too clever for them. He'd watched them from cover, all three, looking slightly cleaner than when he had last met them in that café, but still far from desirable travelling companions, in the train queue. They'd been looking too self-satisfied by half, he thought.

After a while Medinelli slept, and he never noticed the tall man who bumped his way past in the corridor, and who glanced in briefly as he moved on.

The train wasn't too full and Fast and his two companions had a four-seat section to themselves in a coach in the middle of the train. This was rock-bottom-rate travel and most of the other people in the coach looked just about as poverty-stricken as they did. Old women in black shawls, workmen, tired and hungry-looking children being fed on scraps of bread from sleazy shopping-baskets. Some of those people seemed to be carrying all their household possessions in the shopping baskets and the huge parcels and, in a few cases, the dilapidated, bulging suitcases held in by knotted string. Adam Fast's delicate nostrils quivered at the too-close smell of sweat and dirt and grinding poverty. This was going to be a detestable journey, there was no doubt about that, but at least they had got away in safety. And without Medinelli. Taranto offered very good refuge and a nice secure base from which to work. And they had all agreed, once they were safely aboard that train, that no one who mattered had seen their departure. Granted there could have been plain clothes men hanging around the platform on the lookout for Medinelli, but as Fast had remarked earlier, no one would have been watching for *them*.

After a while Adam Fast too dozed off,

snoring gently as the train hurried him to the peaceful indolence of the deep South.

After locating Burgoyne Packard had returned to his seat, casually. Boredom stretched ahead. It was unlikely that Burgoyne would give any trouble on the train; there would presumably be no reason for him to, though Packard's plans did in fact cover the contingency, just in case. For Burgoyne could decide to take a walk and he might spot him and then he might possibly decide to hop off the train at some convenient spot before Taranto. Packard's main pre-occupation therefore was to avoid being seen and recognised, because for one thing he didn't want to flush the man at this stage. Burgoyne had a function to perform and that function wouldn't come into being until they reached Taranto. Packard kept a hat pulled low over his eyes, which made him feel like a tearaway himself, and whenever there was any movement along the aisle he kept his newspaper lifted to cover his face. He was sitting so as to face the direction from which Burgoyne, if he did walk along, would come. So he should be able to spot the man in time if that should happen.

It was difficult, he found after a while, to keep his eyes open. It was a hot, stuffy evening and the air that blew in through the train's window was hot too, bringing in with it all the earthy enervation of the day-long sun on the fields. Opposite him an elderly man slept, his mouth sagging open inelegantly as he snored. There was a strong smell of garlic. Next to the old man was a girl, wakeful still and reading a paperback, with dark hair cut short and her skirt caught up by her reclining position to show off nicely browned thighs. Beside Packard a middle-aged man tried to pretend he wasn't interested, but, glancing sideways from time to time, Packard saw the set look in the eyes and knew precisely where they were focused. Across the aisle was a fat woman with a bad-tempered face, clutching a huge basket firmly on her lap. Packard had already gathered that she was the staring man's wife.

Tedium set in and Packard struggled against his ever-increasing desire to sleep.

After an hour's run, Burgoyne came through, probably to go to the lavatory. Packard lowered his hat into his newspaper, sharply. Burgoyne went on through, lurching with the train. He vanished. Five minutes later he came back. He wasn't aware of Packard sitting so close to him and he went lurching past again. Packard stayed awake, yawning, moving restlessly in his seat. The snoring man woke up. The dark-haired girl fell asleep. The fat woman, noting this, said something sharp to her husband. He grunted irritably and went on watching, perhaps in the hope of seeing more while the girl relaxed in sleep. The train hurried on. A little later and even the staring man's mouth sagged and he too slept, and then astonishingly Adam Fast moved up the aisle from behind and Packard, recognising the man's profile as he went past, forgot all thoughts of weariness and slid his hand inside his jacket for the butt of his Beretta.

NINETEEN

Fast's pudgy body bumped its way along the aisle and vanished into the following coach. He hadn't seen Packard, was probably no more expectant of seeing him than Packard had been of finding

Adam Fast aboard the train. The fact that Fast was here meant that he, Packard, had slipped; the man should have been spotted back at the station. Certainly Packard hadn't expected the show-down to come before Taranto; now it seemed likely that it would. If, that was, Burgoyne happened to spot Adam Fast. Or, presumably, the other way round. For Burgoyne was fairly obviously no longer one of the party and his presence aboard the train was going to be highly unpopular. No one was simply going to let it rest.

Packard wondered why Fast was walking down the train. If this was a visit to the lavatory, he must have walked right past one already—the one Burgoyne had been bound for earlier. But maybe that one had been engaged...Packard decided to hang on a while and watch developments. He looked out of the window; it was dark by this time and the train was moving through a deep valley in the hills; after a longish, slow climb it was gathering speed again. Packard listened to the rhythm of the wheels on the track...*He's coming along,* they seemed to be saying, *he's coming along, he's coming along...*

Fast was.

He appeared again a couple of minutes later, coming back the other way. His expression was blank, so far as Packard could see in a snatched glance from beneath his hat, but he was moving faster and, Packard felt, with rather more purpose than before. Once again he failed to spot Packard and disappeared through into the next coach ahead.

Packard yawned, stretched, and got slowly to his feet. He stepped carefully over the outstretched legs of the sleeping girl and the stare-eyed man and moved out into the aisle. The train was moving at a pretty high speed now, probably going downhill. Packard walked through towards the rear of the train, to where he had seen Burgoyne earlier, in the next-but-one coach behind his own.

He was still there; either asleep or pretending to be. There was an empty seat beside him. Packard dropped into it and Burgoyne opened his eyes.

'You,' he said flatly.

'Yes, me. Surprised?'

The man moistened his lips. 'What are you here for?' he asked.

'Three guesses,' Packard said quietly. 'I've got something to tell you.'

'What?'

'Adam Fast is on the train, and I'd be very surprised if he's alone. But then you knew that already, perhaps?'

Burgoyne opened his eyes wide. They were full of bland innocence. 'I had no idea,' he said. 'No idea in the world, Signor Packard.'

'Oh, sure you hadn't! *You*'ve got no interest in that bunch, have you... Medinelli?'

He got a sharp look in return. 'Listen, what you getting at?'

'Just this,' Packard said pleasantly. 'To my way of thinking, Adam Fast took this train *because* he didn't expect to find you on it. Which means he's double-crossing you. And that in turn means that if he finds you here, he isn't going to be very happy. And I believe he has spotted you and that things are due to happen within a very few minutes from now. We don't want any trouble aboard the train, Medinelli.'

'There won't be any,' the man said, but he didn't sound too confident.

'I hope you're right. I don't want you to start anything. If you have any idea of gunning Adam Fast down—just forget all about it, right?'

'Why should I want to do that?'

Packard said, 'Because I happen to have proof that your real name is Brett Burgoyne. I told you Fast was responsible for what happened to Lois. You're out to get Fast. No, don't try that, Burgoyne.' He grabbed the man's arm, which was sliding into his jacket. He brought out his own gun. 'A little walk, Burgoyne. Just along to the lavatory—that's all. For safety's sake. You'll stay in there till I tell you to come out. Now—move, Burgoyne.'

Slowly, staring at Packard, the man got to his feet. He moved out into the aisle. Packard prodded with his gun. Burgoyne moved along towards the rear of the train and Packard kept very close behind him. They reached the lavatory, found it was engaged. Packard cursed. Burgoyne asked, 'Well? Do we wait—or what?'

He grinned.

Packard was just going to tell him to move on for the next lavatory when someone lurched through from the adjoining coach behind him and as he turned Adam Fast stopped and looked beyond him and said, 'Well, well, Medinelli, this really *is* a surprise, isn't it?'

216

Rollo and Bearsted had been with Adam Fast and after some initial puzzlement and a close scrutiny it hadn't taken Rollo long to tick over. Burgoyne never said a word about Packard's identity, maybe in case Packard should retaliate by giving away his own, but Rollo said, 'Here, d'you know what bloody fish we've landed this time? Mr James flipping Packard!'

While Bearsted kept Burgoyne covered, Fast took a good look. 'Well, Jesus!' he said softly after a moment. 'It's clever all right, but it's still not quite good enough, is it? Not close to. Would you believe it! It's beginning to look like we're going to clean this whole thing up right here and now.' He smiled at Packard. 'I suppose Medinelli's responsible for you being here, isn't he, the dirty double-crossing little—'

Burgoyne said, 'I had nothing to do with it. I didn't know Packard was going to be on the train.'

Fast smiled again, dangerously. 'Never mind, Medinelli, it doesn't make any difference now. You're both going to die very soon. I'm taking no more risks with either of you.' He glanced at his watch. In the half-light his face was threatening, devilish. 'In just ten minutes we're due to pass over the Anconari Gorge. It's a nice long bridge over a nice long drop and the bottom is very, very rocky. There's not going to be a lot left of you, gentlemen, and it's going to be a long time before anyone finds what *is* left. If they do.'

Packard said, 'Just a minute, Fishton. Or Fast if you prefer it. You don't suppose I came on this trip entirely unprepared, do you?'

Fast shrugged. 'If you mean that your disappearance is going to be known when we get to Taranto, it's still going to be too late for you, my dear fellow. You'll be in little pieces by then. And as for myself and my friends...we shall have left the train long before it gets to Taranto and we shall be where no one is going to pick us up.' Once more, he smiled, and this time there was a real gloat in it, a gloat of sheer unassailable confidence. 'Let me put the same question to you that you put to me, Packard: you don't imagine *I* came on this trip unprepared either—do you?' He swung round on Rollo and Bearsted. 'Get them both in the lavatory. We'll be a little more private in there.'

Rollo said, 'It's engaged.'

'Move along to the next, then! You

first, Medinelli. Then you, Rollo. Then Packard. And hurry. And you two—keep your hands away from your pockets. If we pass anyone on the way, act naturally. Or whoever's unlucky enough to get involved, dies too.'

Packard turned to follow on behind Rollo. By this time his gun had been taken away from him but he hadn't yet been frisked. That would come once they were in the privacy of the lavatory. As he walked along he reached up to fend himself off from the train's woodwork; they were moving very fast now and swinging. As he moved his hand it lingered for a moment beneath the lapel of his jacket, then moved away again. Now the train was passing through a tunnel; there was a change in the wheel sounds and dirty, smelly air rushed in through the open windows. They reached the lavatory, found it open, and they all went in. It was a tight fit and there was little room to start anything. Fast locked the door behind them and said, 'Right, Bearsted, you frisk Medinelli. Rollo, you can take Packard.'

He stood in a corner, watchfully. Rollo and Bearsted got to work, sweating in the close atmosphere, making heavy weather of the job. Bearsted removed Burgoyne's gun, found nothing else. Rollo located the tiny transmitter hidden behind Packard's lapel and said, 'What's this, eh?'

'Use your imagination,' Packard snapped.

'It's a radio device,' Rollo said to Fast. He smashed the little disc against the wall. It flew into fragments. 'That's that,' he said, breathing hard. 'Now what?'

Fast looked at his watch again. He said evenly, 'We'll be at the bridge in seven minutes, just about. We'll wait six minutes from now, then I want you to go out and stand by the door to the outside. It's right next to us here. When you hear *this* door opening, you open up your door and stand by to give Medinelli and Packard a farewell wave, right? If anyone comes along, you just give a kind of impatient tap on the lavatory door, see? Like you can't wait. And another as soon as the coast's clear.'

'What if whoever's outside waits too?'

Fast said, 'I told you it's a long bridge. That apart, it'll be up to you to get rid of anyone as quick as you can. Because if you don't, you're going to regret it the rest of your sweet life, Rollo.'

TWENTY

The train rushed on through the tunnel which, like the bridge over the gorge to come, was a long one. The headlights beaming out brilliantly ahead showed the smooth rock walls, the gleaming track. In the cab the driver stared along those beams as though his gaze was riveted to them. His body swayed to the motion of the train; he was like an automaton, scarcely human. He hadn't spoken much to his companion, who was ready to drop off to sleep from sheer boredom.

As the train rounded a bend in the tunnel the driver moved a hand fractionally and very gradually some of the speed came off.

'We are nearing the bridge?'

The driver nodded. 'Yes. A little early, but this does not matter. We may lose a few minutes later on and it is as well to have some time in hand.'

'No doubt...' The policeman yawned, felt that almost overwhelming desire to sleep, might even have succumbed to it if at that very moment the receiver clamped to his ear hadn't given a small click. That brought him awake instantly and he sat up and gave all his attention to his miniature receiver. At first he could make nothing of the sounds that came through to him, they seemed to be nothing but train sounds, and small scratchings, and perhaps, just for a moment, breathing. But no words. It could be that the transmitter had been switched on accidentally, such was by no means impossible...then, when he was starting to lose interest again, he heard, quite distinctly in his ear, the slam of a door and after that a voice. The voice said, 'Right, Bearsted, you frisk Medinelli. Rollo, you can take Packard.' Then, a moment later, another voice said, 'What's this, eh?' and another man answered, 'Use your imagination,' and then, after some further remark that wasn't too clear, there was a loud noise and after that, silence.

'Driver,' the policeman said loudly, 'stop the train!'

The brakes had gone on very suddenly and inside the lavatory they were all thrown violently into one another. As Packard's hand reached up for the communication cord, Fast brought his gun smashing down hard on his wrist. Blood ran and Packard's whole arm went numb. Fast's face was murderous and he looked as though he was going to use his gun right there and then, but he got control and snapped, 'All right, you bastard, you might just as well have pulled the bloody cord, I suppose. They'd realise after a time we were in here. So we're getting out now.'

Rollo said, 'Look, we'll have the whole train on us—'

'Not if we're quick. If we wait, we will. Right now, the passengers won't have ticked over.'

'Ticked over about what?' Rollo asked, looking bewildered.

'Oh, for Christ's sake...that flipping transmitter was *switched on*...that's why the goddam train's stopped! There'll be a cop up front, don't you see?' Already Fast had the door open. 'Out, the lot of you. Rollo and Bearsted, keep your guns on 'em and head 'em back up the tunnel, far as you can make it. We'll have a bit of a start.'

Moving backwards Rollo went for the exit door and flung it open. He jumped down onto the track and stood with his gun covering the door as the others joined him.

Fast said, 'Well, for Christ's sake.' The train stood clear of the tunnel, right on the bridge. It was a dizzy height and a flimsy-looking structure, a spider's-web of metal. There was a cold wind blowing and they could hear the roar and thunder of water on the move over the rocks, invisible in the deep darkness below them. From ahead there came shouts and then the sound of running feet. Fast seemed to have been caught on the hop this time and he was irresolute, looking this way and that. He said, 'We're too flipping far off the tunnel. We'll never make it.' There was a shake in his voice.

Rollo said, 'We'll have to go over. Climb down the girders.'

'No. I haven't the head for heights. I—I can't.'

The running feet were closing. A hoarse voice shouted, 'Throw down your guns or I shall fire.'

'Make up your mind,' Rollo said urgently. He still had Packard well and truly covered. Just then the man coming down from the front of the train used his gun. Bullets zipped close; he wouldn't be aiming for a hit, not just yet. But the fact of the firing rattled Bearsted, and he whipped round and fired back. That gave Burgoyne his chance. He dropped to the ground close to Bearsted and wrapped his arms round the man's legs, jerked and let go. With a wild desperate shriek Bearsted went over the edge, and just for the briefest moment they could see him through the girders, turning over and over, yelling still, then sight and sound of him came to an end as he spun down in the darkness for the waiting rocks and the storming river. Burgoyne was on his feet now, caring nothing, it seemed, for the policeman who was closing in, though slowly now and keeping in such cover as he could; caring nothing either for Fast's gun. He stepped towards the fat man. 'All right, you bastard, you wanted me,' he said thickly, 'and now you've got me. Only not quite the way you wanted. I'm not Medinelli at all—the name's Brett Burgoyne—all right? And now I'm going to smash you, Mr Adam Fast.' He reached out for Fast's throat. 'Just like you killed my girl.' Fast pressed the trigger of his gun and Burgoyne went down on the tracks. His chest was a mess. Packard ducked and grabbed for Rollo's gun and wrenched it from the man's grip. But he wasn't quite quick enough to stop Adam Fast, who turned and ran, ran like a hare towards the mouth of the tunnel, his fear of the height temporarily gone, dodging the fire from Packard's gun and the policeman's, dodging between two coaches to come out on the other side of the train and continue running into the dark night.

TWENTY-ONE

The policeman had joined up with Packard now. Packard had immobilised Rollo for the time being by smashing a fist into his face. Men and women and children looked fearfully out of the windows of the train and there was a shrill buzz of conversation. 'Keep inside,' the policeman called. 'There is a dangerous man around, a murderer. He will not hesitate to shoot. Keep your heads down. We shall catch him.' He bent and slid a pair of handcuffs over Rollo's wrists, then turned him over to the train crew.

'Do you want any help in the search?' the driver asked.

Packard answered for the policeman. 'Thanks, but no,' he said. 'We don't want any unarmed men on this. As our friend said—Fast is dangerous. You'd better leave him to us.' He turned to the policeman. 'Where's the nearest patrol—did you make contact with anyone?'

The policeman nodded. 'Yes, *Signore,* I established contact with a patrol car from Matera and another from Potenza. They are making for the nearest place where the road meets the railway—this is about ten miles ahead, however, so—'

'So it's up to us,' Packard said. He stared into the darkness towards the tunnel. 'We'd better get right on with it, in that case.'

They went ahead slowly and carefully, making as little sound as they could, and near the rear of the train they found the body of the guard. Fast had used a knife on him, seemed almost to have disembowelled him in his panic rage, his desire not only to get clear away but also not to be taken on that high bridge. Once beyond the coaches, Packard and the policeman were in total darkness. There was no moon, no glimmering yet of dawn. Coming off the bridge, away from the rising thunder of the water below, they approached the mouth of the tunnel. Packard felt the hair lifting on his scalp. Each step towards that tunnel was a sheer effort of will. Every small sound in the night made them start, and pause, and listen out more than ever. In the tunnel were dry rustlings, the movement-sounds of tiny night animals that scampered or slithered away from their footsteps. You could have sliced right through that darkness, Packard thought. It was almost a physical presence, unnerving and threatening. At any moment all they might see would be the flash of Fast's gun and that would be their lot. There must, surely, be some loom of light outlining the tunnel entry from the sight of anyone within, a faint lightening that would give the hidden man an excellent target. But still there was no sound, no movement, no attack.

Just nothing.

They moved on, dead slow.

Packard whispered, 'He must be quite close. No one's running, we'd hear anyone a mile off, and he couldn't have got all that far in the time.'

'I agree, *Signore,*' the policeman whispered back. He was fingering a torch, but that was something neither of them was particularly anxious to use. 'I would suggest, *Signore,* that we go not very much farther ahead, say only a few hundred yards...and then sweep back this way again. One on each side of the tunnel, from now on.'

'Okay,' Packard said. 'I'm with you.'

They separated, then carried on. They moved slowly still, with the double set of rails between them now. When he reckoned they had gone far enough Packard gave a low whistle and they turned. It seemed fairly likely that Fast must have lost his gun when he panicked and this was why he'd used the knife on the train guard. The thought didn't make him feel any easier; he hated the idea of steel sliding suddenly between his shoulder-blades. They moved back for the entrance, slowly still, each of them moving along close to the tunnel walls on his own side, reaching out, stumbling over heaps of small stones and rubble. They investigated, as they had done on the inward journey, all the shallow bays used by the track gangs for refuge when trains came through. They found nothing.

By now the faint lightening of the dawn had come and very gradually the tunnel mouth was beginning to take shape. It was when they had still another couple of hundred yards to cover that Packard became aware of a trembling in the rails on his side and almost at the same time heard the distant train sounds and then the piercing whistle from a fast-moving engine. At once he ran across the track to join the policeman on the other set of rails and only seconds after he had done so they saw the gleam of light ahead, the headlamp beam gathering speed towards the tunnel as it came clear of the bridge. And then they saw the man ahead, leaping along the tracks in the beam of light, as scared as a rabbit, racing down towards the tunnel mouth, totally unnerved now. Light from the windows flickered on the running figure as the train roared past them, dinning at their ears, tearing at their bodies with its attendant gale of wind, sending up sparks and dirt that blinded them. The figure was still visible and Packard fired towards it, but it was well out of range and he might as well have saved the effort. They ran ahead quickly but they had lost the man when they emerged from the tunnel. Then the policeman picked him up again. He pointed down the embankment. Fast was rolling down, arms and legs flailing in an effort to check himself. Reaching the bottom, he lay still for a moment and then pulled himself to his feet, lurching and staggering. Looking up he saw the two men. He yelled something they couldn't catch, waved his fists in the air, then started moving towards the network of girders where the bridge structure met the high bank of the gorge.

'What can he be doing?' the policeman asked. He lifted his gun.

Packard said, 'No, don't shoot. He can't get away now. And I'd sooner he was brought in alive. He's rather badly wanted, back in Britain.' Packard thought of Lois Chailey, and the train guard. There were others too. Death by shooting wasn't quite bad enough for any man like Adam Fast. A nice long time in prison would be much worse to a man with Fast's tastes. Besides, a long chat with him might help to write off a few unsolved crimes.

'But it is the only way,' the policeman said.

Packard shook his head. 'No. I'll go in myself and get him. I don't quite get what he's doing...he said he was dead scared of heights, but I suppose anything's better than being taken when it really comes to the crunch.'

'That is true in my experience, yes. Nevertheless, the man cannot possibly hope to avoid capture now. We are here, the bridge is manned, men from the train can be sent if necessary to the other side.'

'He's acting out of panic,' Packard said. 'He's just not reasoning any more.' He pushed the Beretta back into its holster and started scrambling down the embankment, sliding and slithering on the tufty grass, heading diagonally for Adam Fast who had now reached the bridge structure and was pulling himself up the metal, feverishly.

Half an hour later there was a good deal more light and Packard was well out across the long drop with Fast still some twenty feet ahead. By this time Fast had stuck. He was whimpering like a baby and hadn't the guts left to continue with whatever it was his maddened mind had told he might be able to achieve. He was wedged in an angle of one of the big cross-girders, about thirty feet below the track above and some eight hundred feet from the surge of pounding water cascading over the jagged black rocks. Looking up, Packard could see the white, anxious faces of the train's passengers, lining the bridge parapet to watch.

He called out to Fast. 'Hang on,' he told the man. 'Just don't move. And don't look down. Try to relax.'

There was no reply, but he was near enough now to see the gleam of stark terror in the eyes and the crazed set of the mouth. He moved on along the steel girders. A rising wind sighed through the structure, tugging at his clothing, and a few moments later he felt rain. It increased to a sudden heavy downpour that lashed at him, blown along the wind. The steel became slippery and at one point he felt himself going, sliding down one of the girders. It was a bad moment, but he stopped the slide and hung on for a few moments, getting his balance and his confidence back. Now he was within arm's reach of Adam Fast.

He said, 'Take a grip and stop whining. I'm going to get you up, but I can't exactly carry you.'

233

'You won't get me up, Packard. I'll never make it.'

Packard grinned. 'Want to spend the rest of your life here, do you? It's going to be very wet and cold soon.'

The eyes gleamed. There was a curious red fleck in them now. 'I tell you...I can't move. What good d'you think you're doing, for Christ's sake?'

'I suppose I just thought I might impart a little courage. A little confidence. You're tough enough when you're behind a gun, Fast. Or when dealing with a man who's tied down. Or a girl. Try and show some of that spirit now, Fast.'

Fast swore, viciously, into the rising wind. Below them, the river leapt, rushing on its way to the distant sea. They were wet through now. Fast was shivering, his face was white and drawn, and any moment now he might give in, let go and fall. That hadn't to happen. Packard tried again. He said, 'Look, I'm not leaving you here. If necessary I'll knock you out and hold you till someone else comes down. Before long, Fast, you're coming up whatever you may think at this moment. And that's a promise. You may just as well do it now, and do the equivalent of coming quietly. Sometimes, that helps. As you ought to know, with your record.'

Fast said suddenly, 'I can't hang on. Quick, for God's sake!'

Packard moved in closer as he saw the man's grip slackening on the girder. He shifted his body on to the same girder and inched sideways towards the angle where Fast was lying. Just in time he caught the swift change in the man's expression, saw the glint of the dawn's increasing light on the steel blade of the knife as it swooped in towards his back. He let go with his left hand and swung his arm savagely, with all his strength. In the moment that the blade pricked in between his shoulder-blades his arm slashed across Fast's with numbing force and he twisted round sharply and grabbed for the wrist. He put on the pressure and the fingers opened. The knife fell onto the flat surface of the girder and he had grabbed it up before it could fall into the long drop beneath.

With a savage grin on his face he said, 'Right, Mr Adam Fast, you seem to like knives, don't you? Get on your feet and start climbing or you're going to get this where it'll hurt without killing. You're not the only man around here who knows how to do that kind of thing. Well—which is it to be?'

Whimpering again, and shaking like a leaf, Fast climbed to his knees, almost fell, gave a shriek and grabbed for his life at a steel upright. Packard said, 'That's much better. On your way now—and don't stop unless you want a punctured rear end. I'll be right behind you.'

It was a nightmare climb but they made it and as Adam Fast reached the top of the girders beneath the rails, hands helped him through and deposited him in a whining, terrified bundle on the track, where he could see what he had just missed. Handcuffs were snapped over his wrists and he was lifted and dumped aboard the train, where, with Rollo, he was locked into the luggage compartment with the body of the guard and with the armed policeman. A radio report was sent ahead and the train got on the move and ten miles farther on beyond the bridge it was waved down again where the road met the track and where two police cars were waiting. Rollo and Fast were taken off and put in the cars and Packard and the policeman went with them. They headed out for Potenza where a car from Naples took them over. Three hours later Felicity Teal met them in Malfa's office. She said, 'James, I just couldn't wait when I heard what had been happening. Are you all right?'

'Yes,' he said, smiling, 'there's nothing wrong that a bath and a meal and a drink and a night's sleep won't cure. All well your end?'

She nodded. 'It's been a quiet life since you caught that train. Nothing's happened. Oh—except Forbes just rang.'

'He would. What did he want?'

She said, 'He wanted to know what you proposed doing about Lois Chailey. The body, James.'

He said quietly, 'I don't believe there's anyone back home who'll even want to know. She had no family, and Burgoyne's dead. Why shouldn't we leave her where she could have been happy if things had been different?'

'In Naples?'

'Yes,' he said. 'In Naples. I can see to the formalities myself. It's bound to be difficult in the circumstances, but surely not impossible.' He was silent for a while then he asked, 'Anything else he wanted?'

'He wanted to know if you'd got a line on Burgoyne's share of the Hatton Garden loot.'

'Burgoyne died a little too suddenly to be asked, so the answer's no. We'll need to do a little more work on that chap Kilroe, the one in Parkhurst. There's just a chance his memory could be revived after all, I suppose.'

He felt her anxiety reaching out to him as she asked, 'Does this mean you'll have to go back inside, James?'

He smiled. 'I hope not!'

'So do I,' she said. Then she added, 'By the way, Forbes said there was no hurry to see us so far as he was concerned and subject to your reporting in full by telephone, we could take a few days leave if we wanted to.'

'Uh-huh. And what did you say...h'm?'

'I said I—I did want to.' She looked up at him. 'Okay with you?'

'Very okay with me,' he said, and kissed her.

The publishers hope that this book has given you enjoyable reading. Large Print Books are especially designed to be as easy to see and hold as possible. If you wish a complete list of our books, please ask at your local library or write directly to: Dales Print Books, Long Preston, North Yorkshire, BD23 4ND, England.